A REVIVED
M O D E R N
C L A S S I C

THE COMFORTERS

ALSO BY MURIEL SPARK

AVAILABLE FROM NEW DIRECTIONS

The Driver's Seat

The Public Image

MURIEL SPARK
THE COMFORTERS

A NEW DIRECTIONS BOOK

Manufactured in the United States of America
New Directions Books are printed on acid-free paper
First published clothbound by Lippincott in 1957
First published as New Directions Paperbook 796 in 1994

Library of Congress Cataloging in Publication Data

Spark, Muriel.
    The comforters / Muriel Spark.
       p.   cm.—(Revived modern classic)   (New Directions paperbook ; 796)
    ISBN 0-8112-1285-8 (alk. paper)
    1. Catholic converts—Great Britain—Fiction.   2.   Young women—
    Great Britain—Fiction.   3. Women authors—Psychology—Fiction.
    I. Title.   II. Series.
    PR6037.P29C6   1994
    823'.914—dc20   94-12825
                                                           CIP

New Directions Books are published for James Laughlin
by New Directions Publishing Corporation,
80 Eighth Avenue, New York 10011

To Alan and Edwina Barnsley
With Love

PART ONE

Chapter 1

ON the first day of his holiday Laurence Manders woke to hear his grandmother's voice below.

'I'll have a large wholemeal. I've got my grandson stopping for a week, who's on the B.B.C. That's my daughter's boy, Lady Manders. He won't eat white bread, one of his fads.'

Laurence shouted from the window, 'Grandmother, I adore white bread and I have no fads.'

She puckered and beamed up at him.

'Shouting from the window,' she said to the baker.

'You woke me up,' Laurence said.

'My grandson,' she told the baker. 'A large wholemeal, and don't forget to call on Wednesday.'

Laurence looked at himself in the glass. 'I must get up,' he said, getting back into bed. He gave himself seven minutes.

He followed his grandmother's movements from the sounds which came clearly through the worn cottage floorboards. At seventy-eight Louisa Jepp did everything very slowly but with extreme attention, as some do when they know they are slightly drunk. Laurence heard a clink and a pause, a tinkle and a pause, breakfast being laid. Her footsteps clicked like a clock that is running down as she moved between the scullery and the little hot kitchen; she refused to shuffle.

When he was half dressed Laurence opened a tiny drawer on the top of the tall old-fashioned chest. It contained some of his grandmother's things, for she had given him her room. He counted three hairpins, eight mothballs; he found a small piece of black velvet embroidered with jet beads now loose on their thread. He reckoned the bit of stuff would be about two and a half inches by one and a half. In another drawer he found a comb

9

with some of his grandmother's hair on it and noted that the object was none too neat. He got some pleasure from having met with these facts, three hairpins, eight moth-balls, a comb none too neat, the property of his grand-mother, here in her home in Sussex, now in the present tense. That is what Laurence was like.

'It is unhealthy,' his mother had lately told him. 'It's the only unhealthy thing about your mind, the way you notice absurd details, it's absurd of you.'

'That's what I'm like,' Laurence said.

As usual, she knew this meant deadlock, but carried on, 'Well, it's unnatural. Because sometimes you see things that you shouldn't.'

'Such as?'

She did not say, but she knew he had been in her room prying into her messy make-up drawer, patting the little bottles like a cat and naming them. She could never per-suade him that this was wrong. After all, it was a viola-tion of privacy.

Very often Laurence said, 'It would be wrong for you but it isn't for me.'

And always Helena Manders, his mother, would reply 'I don't see that', or 'I don't agree', although really she did in a way.

In his childhood he had terrorized the household with his sheer literal truths.

'Uncle Ernest uses ladies' skin food, he rubs it on his elbows every night to keep them soft' ... 'Eileen has got her pain' ... 'Georgina Hogg has three hairs on her chin when she doesn't pull them out. Georgina has had a letter from her cousin which I read.'

These were memorable utterances. Other items which he aired in the same breath, such as, 'There's been a cob-web on the third landing for two weeks, four days and fifteen hours, not including the time for the making' – these were received with delight or indifference according to mood, and forgotten.

His mother told him repeatedly, 'I've told you repeatedly, you are not to enter the maids' rooms. After all, they are entitled to their privacy.'

As he grew older he learned to conceal the sensational portions of his knowledge, imparting only what was necessary to promote his reputation for being remarkably observant. In those days his father was capable of saying, on the strength of a school report,

'I always knew Laurence would outgrow that morbid phase.'

'Let's hope he has,' Helena Manders had said. Parents change. In those days, Laurence was aware that she half-suspected him of practising some vague sexual perversion which she could not name, would not envisage, and which in any case he did not practise. Then, it was almost to put her at ease, to assure her that he was the same Laurence as of old, that he said, during the holidays of his last term,

'Eileen is going to have a baby.'

'She's a good Catholic girl,' Helena protested; she was herself a Catholic since her marriage. None the less, on challenging Eileen in the kitchen, the case turned out to be so. Eileen, moreover, defiantly refused to name the man. Laurence was able to provide this information.

'I've always kept up with Eileen's correspondence,' he explained. 'It enlivens the school holidays.'

'You've been in that poor girl's room, reading her letters behind her back, the poor thing!'

'Shall I tell you what her boy friend wrote?' Laurence said tyrannously.

'I'm shocked as you know,' she said, accepting that this made no impression. 'How you, a good Catholic − but apart from that, it's illegal, I believe, to read letters addressed to others,' she said, defeated.

Merely to give her the last word he pointed out, 'Well, you've got them married, my dear. A good Catholic marriage. That's the happy result of my shocking perusal of Eileen's letters.'

'The end doesn't justify the means.'

Pat it came out just as he had expected. An answer for everything. All the same, incidents like this helped to deaden the blow when she realized that Laurence was abandoning, and finally had abandoned religion.

Louisa Jepp sat at the table writing out her football pools as she waited for Laurence.

'Come down!' she said to the ceiling, 'and leave off your snooping, dear.'

As soon as he appeared she told him, 'If Manchester City had won last week I should have got thirty thousand.'

Louisa folded her football coupon and placed it under the clock. She gave all her attention to Laurence and his breakfast.

She was half gipsy, the dark one and the youngest of a large red-haired family, which at the time of her birth owed its prosperity to the father's success as a corn dealer. The success was owing to good fortune in the first place, his having broken jail while waiting to come before the Bench, never afterwards returning to his gipsy tribe. It was a hundred and thirty years after this event that Louisa was sitting down to breakfast with Laurence.

Louisa's hair remains black, though there is not much of it. She is short, and seen from the side especially, her form resembles a neat double potato just turned up from the soil with its small round head, its body from which hangs the roots, her two thin legs below her full brown skirt and corpulence. Her face, from the front, is square, receding in planes like a prism. The main lines on her face are deep, they must have been in gradual evidence since she was thirty, they seemed carved to the bone. But the little wrinkles are superficial, brushing the surface of her skin, coming and going like innumerable stars when she puckers a smile or unfolds a look of surprise. Her eyes are deep-set and black. Her hands and feet very small. She wears rimless spectacles. She is still alive, not much changed from that day when Laurence came down to breakfast. She was wearing a brown dress, a brown woollen jacket with gilt buttons, and a pair of diamond earrings embedded in her ears.

When Laurence had sized her up, as he always did with everyone, he dipped his fork into a jar and drew out something long, white and pickled.

'What can this be?'

'Chid'lings,' she said. 'They are beautiful.'

He was accustomed to Louisa's food: whelks, periwinkles, milts and roes, chitterlings and sweetbreads, giblets, brains and the tripes of ruminating animals. Louisa prepared them at long ease, by many processes of affusion, diffusion and immersion, requiring many pans of brine, many purifications and simmerings, much sousing and sweetening by slow degrees. She seldom bought an ordinary cut or joint, and held that people who went through life ignoring the inward vitals of shells and beasts didn't know what was good for them.

'If you won thirty thousand in the pool, what would you do?' Laurence said.

'Buy a boat,' she replied.

'I would paddle you up and down the river,' Laurence said. 'A houseboat would be nice. Do you remember that fortnight on the houseboat, my first year at prep school?'

'I mean a boat for crossing the sea. Yes, it was lovely on the houseboat.'

'A yacht? Oh, how grand.'

'Well, a good-sized boat,' said Louisa, 'that's what I'd buy. Suitable for crossing the Channel.'

'A motor cruiser,' Laurence suggested.

'That's about it,' she said.

'Oh, how grand.'

She did not reply, for he had gone too far with his 'Oh, how grand!'

'We could do the Mediterranean,' he said.

'Oh, how grand,' she said.

'Wouldn't it be more fun to buy a house?' Laurence had just remembered his mother's plea, 'If you get an opportunity do try to persuade her to take a little money from us and live comfortably in her own house.'

She answered, 'No. But if I won a smaller sum I'd buy this cottage. I'm sure Mr Webster would sell.'

'Oh, I'd love to think of you having the cottage for your very own. Smugglers Retreat is such a dear little house.' Even as he spoke Laurence knew that phrases like 'your very own' and 'dear little house' betrayed what he was leading up to, they were not his grandmother's style.

'I know what you're leading up to,' said Louisa. 'Help yourself to the cigarettes.'

'I have my own. Why won't you let father buy the cottage for you? He can afford it.'

'I manage very nicely,' said Louisa. 'Smoke one of these – they come from Bulgaria.'

'Oh, how grand!' But he added, 'How extremely smart and where did you get them from?'

'Bulgaria. I think through Tangiers.'

Laurence examined the cigarette. His grandmother, a perpetual surprise. She rented the cottage, lived as an old-age pensioner.

Her daughter Helena said frequently, 'God knows how she manages. But she always seems to have plenty of everything.'

Helena would tell her friends, 'My mother won't accept a penny. Most independent; the Protestant virtues, you know. God knows how she manages. Of course, she's half gipsy, she has the instinct for contriving ways and means.'

'Really! Then you have gipsy blood, Helena? Really, and you so fair, how romantic. One would never have thought –'

'Oh, it comes out in me sometimes,' Helena would say.

It was during the past four years, since the death of her husband, penniless, that Louisa had revealed, by small tokens and bit by bit, an aptitude for acquiring alien impenetrable luxuries.

Manders' Figs in Syrup, with its seventy-year-old trademark – an oriental female yearning her draped form towards, and apparently worshipping a fig tree – was the only commodity that Louisa was willing to accept from her daughter's direction. Louisa distributed the brown sealed jars of this confection among her acquaintance; it kept them in mind of the living reality underlying their verbal tradition, 'Mrs Jepp's daughter was a great beauty, she married into Manders' Figs in Syrup.'

'Tell your father,' said Louisa, 'that I have not written to thank him because he is too busy to read letters. He will like the Bulgarian cigarettes. They smell very high. Did he like *my* figs?'

'Oh yes, he was much amused.'

'So your mother told me when she wrote last. Did he *like* them?'

'Loved them, I'm sure. But we were awfully tickled.'

Louisa, in her passion for pickling and preserving, keeps up with the newest methods. Some foods go into jars, others into tins sealed by her domestic canning machine. When Louisa's own figs in syrup, two cans of them with neatly pencilled labels, had arrived for Sir Edwin Manders, Helena had felt uneasy at first.

'Is she having a lark with us, Edwin?'

'Of course she is.'

Helena was not sure what sort of a lark. She wrote to Louisa that they were all very amused.

'Did they enjoy the figs?' Louisa pressed Laurence.

'Yes, they were lovely.'

'They are as good as Manders', dear, but don't tell your father I said so.'

'Better than Manders',' Laurence said.

'Did you taste some, then?'

'Not actually. But I know they were most enjoyable, Mother said' (which Helena had not said).

'Well, that's what I sent them for. To be enjoyed. You shall have some later. I don't know what they are talking about – "much amused". Tell your father that I'm giving him the cigarettes for enjoyment, tell him that, my dear.'

Laurence was smoking his Bulgarian. 'Most heady,' he

said. 'But Mother takes a fit when you send expensive presents. She knows you have to deny yourself and –'

He was about to say 'pinch and scrape', using his mother's lamenting words; but this would have roused the old lady. Besides, the phrase was obviously inaccurate; his grandmother was surrounded by her sufficiency, always behind which hovered a suspicion of restrained luxury. Even her curious dishes seemed chosen from an expansive economy of spirit rather than any consideration of their cost in money.

'Helena is a sweet girl, but she does deceive herself. I'm not in need of anything, as she could very well see, if she took the trouble. There is no need for Helena to grieve on my account.'

Laurence was away all day, with his long legs in his small swift car, gone to look round and about the familiar countryside and coastline, gone to meet friends of his own stamp and education, whom he sometimes brought back to show off to them his funny delicious grandmother. Louisa Jepp did many things during that day. She fed the pigeons and rested. Rather earnestly, she brought from its place a loaf of white bread, cut the crust off one end, examined the loaf, cut another slice, and looked again. After the third slice she began at the other end, cutting the crust, peering at the loaf until, at the fourth slice, she smiled at what she saw, and patting the slices into place again put back the loaf in the tin marked 'bread'.

At nine o'clock Laurence returned. The sitting-room which looked out on the village was very oblong in shape. Here he found his grandmother with visitors, three men. They had been playing rummy, but now they were taking Louisa's refreshments, seated along each side of the room. One was in an invalid chair; this was a young man, not more than twenty-four.

'Mr Hogarth, my grandson; my grandson, Mr Webster; and this is *young* Mr Hogarth. My grandson is on the B.B.C., my daughter's son, Lady Manders. You've heard him give the commentaries on the football and the races, Laurence Manders.'

'Heard you last Saturday.' This was Mr Webster, the oldest guest, almost as old as Louisa.

'Saw you this morning,' Laurence said.

Mr Webster looked surprised.

'With the baker's van,' Laurence added.

Louisa said, 'Laurence is very observant, he has to be for his job.'

Laurence, who was aglow from several drinks, spoke the obliging banality, 'I never forget a face', and turning to the elder Hogarth he said, 'For instance, I'm sure I've seen your face somewhere before.' But here, Laurence began to lose certainty. 'At least – you resemble someone I know but I don't know who.'

The elder Hogarth looked hopelessly at Louisa, while his son, the boy in the invalid chair, said, 'He looks like me. Have you seen me before?'

Laurence looked at him.

'No,' he said, 'I haven't. Nobody at all like you.'

Then, in case he should have said the wrong thing, considering the young man was a cripple, Laurence rattled on.

'I may take up detective work one of these days. It would be quite my sort of thing.'

'Oh no, you could never be a detective, Laurence,' Louisa said, very seriously.

'Now, why not?'

'You have to be cunning to be a detective. The C.I.D. are terribly sly and private detectives will stoop to anything. You aren't a bit sly, dear.'

'I notice extraordinary things,' Laurence boasted casually, lolling his brown head along the back of the sofa. 'Things which people think are concealed. Awful to be like that, isn't it?'

Laurence had the feeling that they didn't like him, they suspected him. He got nervous, and couldn't seem to say anything right. They more and more seemed not to like him as he went on and on compulsively about the wonderful sleuth he would make. And all the time he was talking he actually was taking them in, sleuth-like.

Their presence in his grandmother's house was strange and surprising, and for that reason alone did not really surprise him. Louisa is pouring out tea. She calls the young Hogarth 'Andrew'. His father is 'Mervyn' to her. Webster is 'Mr Webster'.

Mr Webster with his white hair, white moustache and dark nautical jacket is not easy to identify with his early-morning appearance – the tradesman in a sandy-brown overall who calls with the bread: Laurence felt pleased with himself for recognizing Mr Webster, who wore brown suede shoes, size ten by Laurence's discernment, whose age might be going on seventy-five, and who, by his voice, is a Sussex man.

Mervyn Hogarth was thin and small. He had a washed-out sandy colouring. Louisa had prepared for him a thin slice of brown bread and butter.

'Mervyn has to eat often, in small snacks, for his gastric trouble,' Louisa explained. By his speech, the elder Hogarth is a knowing metropolitan product. God knows what he is doing at Louisa's, why he is on sufficiently familiar visiting terms for first names and gastric confidences. But Laurence was not a wonderer. He observed that the elder Hogarth wore unpressed flannels and an old ginger tweed jacket with the air of one who can afford to go careless. The son Andrew, with full red lips, was square and large-faced with glasses. He was paralysed in the legs.

As Louisa asked Laurence, 'Did you have a nice outing, dear?' Andrew winked at him.

Laurence resented this, an injustice to his grandmother. He felt averse to entering a patronizing conspiracy with Andrew against the old lady; he was on holiday for a special reason connected with a love affair, he wanted a change from the complications of belonging to a sophisticated social group. The grandmother refreshed him, she was not to be winked about. And so Laurence smiled at

Andrew, as if to say, 'I acknowledge your wink. I cannot make it out at all. I take it you mean something pleasant.'

Andrew started looking round the room; he seemed to have missed something that should be there. At last he fixed on the box of Bulgarian cigarettes on Louisa's sideboard; reaching out he opened the box and helped himself to one. Mr Webster tried to exchange a glance with Louisa disapproving of her guest's manners, but she would not be drawn in to it. She rose and passed the open box to Laurence.

Andrew told him, 'They are Bulgarian.'

'Yes, I know. Rather odd, aren't they?'

'They grow on one,' Andrew remarked.

'Bulgarian!' his father exclaimed. 'I must try one!'

Louisa silently passed the cigarettes. She inclined her head demurely towards Laurence, acknowledging an unavoidable truth: the fact that three stubbed-out fat Bulgarian ends already lay in the ash-tray beside Mervyn Hogarth's chair.

Louisa sat passively witnessing Hogarth's performance as he affected to savour a hitherto untried brand of cigarette.

'My dear Louisa, how exotic! I don't think I could cope with many of these. So strong and so ... what shall I say?'

'Pungent,' said Louisa patiently, as one who has heard the same word said before by the same man in the same place.

'*Pungent*,' Mervyn repeated, as if she had hit on the one only precise word.

He continued, 'A flavour of – the Balkans, a tang as of – of –'

Louisa obliged him again, 'Goats' milk.'

'That's it! Goats' milk.'

Louisa's black shiny buttons of eyes turned openly on Laurence. He was watching the man's face; he glanced towards the ash-tray with its evidence of the pose, then looked at Mervyn again. Louisa began to giggle inaudibly as if she were gently shaking a bottle of cough-mixture within herself. Mr Webster caught her movement with the corner of his eye. From where he was seated, and his neck being stiff, he had to swivel round from the waist to get a better view of Louisa. At this sign, her face puckered slightly, but presently she composed herself like a school-girl.

Laurence said to Andrew, 'Do you live round here?'

Father and son replied simultaneously. Mervyn said, 'Oh, no'; Andrew said, 'Oh, yes.'

Louisa's mirth got the better of her, and though her lips were shut tight she whinnied through her nose like a pony. Mr Webster clicked his cup into his saucer as if the walls had spoken.

The Hogarths immediately attempted to rectify their blunder. Both started together again – Mervyn: 'Well, we live in London mostly –' Andrew: 'I mean, we're here most of the time –' The father decided to let Andrew take over.

'And we sometimes go abroad,' he concluded limply.

Laurence looked at his watch, and said hastily to Andrew, 'Coming for a drink? There's about fifteen minutes to closing.' Then he saw his blunder. For the moment the boy had looked quite normal, not a cripple at all.

'Not tonight thanks. Another time, if you're staying,' Andrew said, unsurprised.

'Laurence is stopping till the end of the week,' said Louisa.

Laurence hurried out. They could hear his footsteps crossing the quiet road and down the village street to-wards the Rose and Crown.

Mr Webster spoke. 'Charming boy.'

Louisa said, 'Yes, and so clever.'

'Interesting lad,' Mervyn said.

'I was wondering . . .' said Andrew.

'What, dear?' Louisa asked him.

'Hadn't we better clear off till next week?'

Mr Webster twisted round to face the old lady. 'Mrs Jepp,' he said, 'I did not think you would permit your grandson meeting us. I understood he was to be out this evening. I trust he will not be upset in any way.'

'My!' said Louisa graciously. 'He won't be upset, Mr Webster. Young people are very democratic these days.'

That was not what had been meant. Mervyn spoke next.

'I think he will ask questions. It's only natural, Louisa, after all, what do you expect?' He lit one of the Bulgarian cigarettes.

'Whatever questions should he ask?'

'He is bound to wonder....' said Andrew.

'He's bound to ask who we are, what we're doing here,' said Mervyn.

Mr Webster looked sadly at Mervyn, pained by some crudity in the other's words.

'My!' said Louisa. 'Laurence will certainly ask all about you. Would you care for another game, gentlemen?'

Mervyn looked at the clock.

Andrew said, 'He'll be back after the pub closes, won't he?'

Mr Webster smiled paternally at Louisa. 'The matter is not urgent,' he said, 'we can leave our business till the end of the week, if you know of an evening when your grandson will be out.'

'It can be discussed in front of Laurence,' she said. 'Laurence is a dear boy.'

'Of course,' said Mervyn.

'That's just what we mean,' said Andrew. 'The dear boy shouldn't be made to wonder –'

Louisa looked a little impatient. Something was defeating her. 'I did hope,' she said, 'that we could avoid making any difference between Laurence and ourselves. I assure you, with discretion we could say all we want to say in Laurence's presence. He has not got a suspicious nature.'

'Ah, discretion,' Mr Webster said, 'my dear Mrs Jepp, discretion is always desirable.'

Louisa beamed warmly at him, as at one who had come nearest to understanding her.

Mervyn spoke. 'I understand you, Louisa. You can't bear to participate in separated worlds. You have the instinct for unity, for coordinating the inconsistent elements of experience; you have the passion for picking up the idle phenomena of life and piecing them together. That is your ideal, it used to be mine. Reality, however, refuses to accommodate the idealist. It is difficult at your age to grasp a fact which you have never had occasion to recognize, but –'

'I don't know what you mean,' Louisa said, 'not at any age I wouldn't know.'

'Of course.'

'You are too far away,' she said, but then she perked up, 'Now Mervyn, if you feel I'm too old-fashioned in my ways I will quite understand. You may always withdraw from our arrangements.'

Mervyn, who had stood up, sat down again. Andrew gave an unsmiling laugh which caused Louisa to look at him with surprise.

Andrew responded: 'He spoke about doing detective work. He seems to be quite smart in the head.'

'Laurence is doing nicely on the wireless. He would never make a detective, nothing so low.'

'He would make a good informer,' Andrew said, and from the privilege of his invalid chair looked squarely at her.

'My, you need not continue with us, Andrew dear, if anything troubles you. In which case, of course, *we* shouldn't continue, should we?' She looked at Mervyn and Mr Webster, but they did not answer. They rose then, to leave. As he took her hand Mr Webster said, 'You see, Mrs Jepp, your dear grandson *is* exceedingly observant. That was the only reason I had for questioning the wisdom.'

Louisa laughed, 'Oh, he never misses anything. I've never met anyone like him for getting the details.

But, you know, the dear boy can't put two and two together.'

'You mean,' said Mervyn, 'that he lacks the faculty of reflection?'

'I mean,' said Laurence's grandmother, 'that he could be more intelligent in some ways than he is. But he's clever enough to get on in the world, and he has a sweet nature, that's what matters.'

'And if he asks any questions ...' said Andrew.

'Oh, he *will* ask questions,' Louisa answered him.

There was no doing anything with her.

'Oh, Mrs Jepp, you will be discreet won't you? I'm sure you will,' said Mr Webster.

'My grandson can't put two and two together – not so's to make four.' She looked rather amused so as to make them rather uncomfortable.

'He's leaving on Friday?' Mervyn asked.

'Yes, I'm afraid so '

'Friday evening then?' said Mervyn.

'Yes,' she answered with melancholy.

'See you Friday,' said Andrew.

'Thank you, Mrs Jepp, for a most pleasant evening,' said Mr Webster.

Because Laurence had started writing a letter, resting the paper on a book on his knee, Louisa was clearing part of the table for him, saying, 'Come, love, sit up at the table, it's more comfortable.'

'No, I always write like this.'

Louisa spread a white cloth over the corner reserved for Laurence.

'Always put a white cloth under your papers when you write a letter. It's good for your eyes because it reflects back the light. Come, dear, sit up at the table.'

Laurence shifted to the table and continued writing. After a few minutes he said, 'The white cloth does make a difference. Much pleasanter.'

Louisa, lying full-length on the sofa by the little back

window where she rested till tea-time in the afternoons, replied dozily, 'When I told Mervyn Hogarth of that little trick, he started working out in his head whether it could be effective or not, all about light-rays and optics. "Try it, Mervyn," I said, "just try it, then you'll know for certain that I'm right."'

'Of course,' Laurence reflected absently, 'it may be due to something psychological.'

'Oh, it's something psychological all right,' said Louisa surprisingly and imponderably. Then she closed her eyes.

She opened them again a few seconds later to say, 'If it's your mother you're writing to give her my love.'

'I'm writing to Caroline, actually.'

'Then give her my love and say I hope she feels better than she was at Easter. How has she been lately?'

'Miserable. She's gone away to some religious place in the north for a rest.'

'She won't get much of a rest in a religious place.'

'That's what I thought. But this is one of Mother's ideas. She gets together with her priests and builds these buildings. Then they dedicate them to a saint. Then mother sends her friends to stay in them.'

'But Caroline isn't a Catholic.'

'She's just become one.'

'I *thought* she was looking thin. How does that affect you, dear?'

'Well, of course Caroline's left me, in a way. At least, she's gone to live somewhere else.'

'Well!' said the old woman, 'that's a nice thing!'

'We might get married some day.'

'Ah, and if not?' She looked at him with a reserved wonder as she added, 'Does Caroline know what she's doing? The one certain way for a woman to hold a man is to leave him for religion. I've known it happen. The man might get another girl, but he never can be happy with anyone else after a girl has left him for religious reasons. *She* secures him for good.'

'Is that really true?' Laurence said. 'How very jolly. I must tell Caroline.'

'Oh well, my love, it's all for the best. I hope you can marry her, soon. They wouldn't make you become a Catholic, you only have to promise to bring up the children Catholics. And after all, children these days make up their own minds when they grow up. And there's nothing wrong in being a Catholic if you want to be one.'

'It's a bit complicated,' Laurence said. 'Poor Caroline isn't well.'

'Poor Caroline. That's religion for you. Give her my love and tell her to come down here. I'll feed her up, I daresay everything will come out all right.'

'Grandmother has just dozed off again,' Laurence wrote, 'after looking up to inquire after you. The news of your conversion caused a serious expression, on her face. Made her look like one of Rembrandt's old women, but she rapidly regained her Louisa face. She wants you here, to give you things to eat.

'I hated seeing your train out at Euston and mooned off afterwards with thoughts of following you on the evening train. Met the Baron in Piccadilly Underground and walking back with him to the bookshop fell under his influence and decided against. He argued, "The presence of a non-believer in a Catholic establishment upsets them if the unbeliever is not interested in acquiring their faith. Those places always advertise their welcome to the faithless. However, if you go merely looking for Caroline, it will upset them, you will not be welcome. Moreover, they will have it in for Caroline, for being manifestly more desirable to you than their faith." On the whole, I decided it would be cloddish to barge in, just as well as it has turned out.

'I couldn't face the flat so went over to Hampstead. Father was in, Mother out. He let fall something that rather worries me. Apparently there's a woman by name of Hogg at the outfit you are staying at. She's a sort of manageress. Mother got her the job. God knows why. We all loathe her. That's why we've always gone out of our way for her really. She's that Georgina Hogg I think I've mentioned, the one who used to be a kind of nursery-governess before we went to school. She got married but her husband left her. Poor bastard, no wonder. We used to feel sorry for him. She suffers from chronic righteous-ness, exerts a sort of moral blackmail. Mother has a con-science about her – about hating her so much I mean, is terrified of her but won't admit it. Father calls her Man-ders' Mortification. Of course she's harmless really if you don't let her get under your skin. I think I could handle the woman, at least I used to. But best to avoid her, darling. I hope you won't come across her. I confronted mother with her damned silliness in sending you to a place where Georgina is, at a time when you're feeling limp. She looked a bit guilty but said, "Oh, Caroline will put Georgina in her place." I do hope you will. If she upsets you, leave immediately and come down here to be plumped up. Such things are happening down here!

'Arrived on Sunday night. My little grandmother is a mighty woman, as I always knew. I've discovered such things! She runs a *gang*. I'm completely in the dark as to what sort of gang, but I should probably think they are Communist spies. Three men. A father and son. The son's a cripple, poor chap. The father has a decided air of one *manqué*. The third gangster is rather a love, like a retired merchant sailor, fairly old. He's sweet on Grand-mother. He owns the local bakery and delivers the bread himself.

'I don't know how far Grandmother is implicated in their activities, but she's certainly the boss. She's hand-somely well-off. I think she only draws her pension to avoid suspicion. Do you know where she keeps her capital? In the *bread*. She sticks diamonds in the bread. Without a word of exaggeration, I came across a loaf weirdly cut at both ends, and in one end diamonds, real ones. I won-dered what the hell they were at first, and picked out one of the stones ever so carefully. Diamonds look so different when they aren't set in jewellery. When I saw what it was, I put the stone back in its place. Grandmother has no idea that I'm on to this, of course. Isn't she a wonder? I wonder what her racket is. I don't think seriously of course that they are spies, but criminals of some sort. The thing is, Grandmother isn't being used, she's running the show. The main thing is, Mother mustn't find out, so be most careful, my love, what you say.

'I intend to find everything out, even if it means taking an extra week and mucking up Christmas. I've started compiling a dossier.

'Any ideas on the subject, let me know. Personally, I think Grandmother is having the time of her life, but it might be serious for her if the men are caught. I can't begin to guess what they'd be caught at. They may be jewel thieves, but that doesn't fit in with the sweet naval old fellow's character. Anything fits G'mother's.

'Grandmother openly refers to them as "my gang", airy as a Soho slender. Says they come to play cards. I met them here the other night, since when I've been snooping. I wish you would come for a few days and help me "put two & two together" as G'mother says. I hope you don't get the jitters at St Philumena's. Take it from me, you have to pick and choose amongst Catholic society in England, the wrong sort can drive you nuts. Mother knows she's done the wrong thing in sending you there. It's her passion for founding "Centres" and peopling them, gets the better of her. Father swears she'll start a schism.

'I expect a letter from you tomorrow. Longing to hear that you have got Mrs Hogg under control. It would be rather fun in a way if you had a set-to with her. I'd like to be there if you did. *There*, but concealed.'

Louisa opened her eyes and said, 'Put the kettle on, dear.'

Laurence laid down his pen. He asked her, 'Who d'you think is in charge of that religious place Caroline's gone to?'

'Who, dear?'

'Mrs Hogg.'

'In charge! I thought it was a convent.'

'No, only a Centre. Georgina is housekeeper or something.'

'Does your mother know that?'

'Yes, she gave her the job.'

'I think something is happening to Helena's mind,' said Louisa.

'Mrs Hogg! Just think of her, Grandmother, worming in on Caroline.'

'Mrs Hogg,' said Louisa, as if she'd never heard the like. 'Mrs Hogg. Well, Caroline will fix her.'

Laurence went into the scullery to fill the kettle, and shouted from there,

'You haven't seen her lately?'

His grandmother was silent. But as he returned and placed the kettle on the black coal stove, Louisa told him,

'I haven't seen her for years. A few months ago your Mother wrote to suggest that Georgina Hogg should come and live here as a companion for me.'

Laurence chuckled.

'You said no bloody fear, I suppose.'

'I said that I would not wish to have that poisonous woman in my house for a five-second visit. It fairly puts you against Catholics, a person like that.'

Laurence took up his pen again.

'I detest that woman,' said Louisa.

'Grandmother is awake now,' Laurence wrote. 'She has been delivering herself of her views on Ma Hogg. "Poisonous" she says. It makes me rather sorry for the old Hogg being so dislikable. Truly, she has to be savoured to be believed.'

'Tell Caroline,' Louisa broke in, 'to be careful of Mrs Hogg. Say she's dangerous.'

'I've told her,' Laurence said.

He finished his letter, and read it over.

After tea he added to it, 'P.S. I forgot to mention Grandmother's cheque book. According to the stubs she donates the exact sum of her pension each week to the Prisoners' Aid Society.'

He sealed the letter, then went to post it.

Chapter 2

A STORM, fierce enough to hold up the shipping at the mouth of the Mersey, ranged far enough inland to keep Caroline Rose indoors, where she paced the pale green corridors. Not for exercise but in order to think. A thinking-place of green corridors. The Pilgrim Centre of St Philumena.

'Taking exercise.' This was Mrs Hogg tacking on to her, infuriating. Taking exercise. Not a question, a statement.

'Good afternoon,' said Caroline.

'And feeling lonely,' said Mrs Hogg with her sort of smile. Feeling lonely, taking exercise. Caroline made no answer. The small perfect idea which had been crystallizing in her mind went all to mist. All right, I am at your disposal. Eat me, bloodywell take the lot. I am feeling lonely. Rome has spoken.

'Another time,' said Mrs Hogg, 'you don't want to make a private Retreat. You want to come in the summer with one of the big pilgrimages for one of the big Feasts.'

'Do I?' Caroline said.

'Yes,' said Mrs Hogg. 'That's what you want to do. Please call me Georgina by the way. I'll call you Caroline. Sometimes we have as many as a hundred and thirty pilgrims to stay. And of course thousands for the day pilgrimages. Sir Edwin and Lady Manders and Father Ingrid had no idea what they started when they started St Philumena's. You must meet the Manders.'

'I know them,' said Caroline.

'Oh, you do. Are you one of their converts? They are always making converts.'

'Converts to what?' said Caroline in the imperative need to be difficult. Caroline vented in her mind her private formula: *You are damned. I condemn you to eternal flames. You are* caput, *as good as finished, you have had it, my dear.* More expressive, and therefore more satisfying than merely 'Go to hell', and only a little less functional than a small boy's 'Bang-bang, you're dead !'

'Converts to the Faith, of course,' Mrs Hogg was saying.

During her three days' stay at St Philumena's she had already observed Mrs Hogg. On her first evening Caroline overheard her:

'You have to take what's put before you here. Sometimes we have as many as a hundred and thirty pilgrims. Suppose a hundred and thirty people all wanted tea without milk –'

Her victim, a young lawyer who was recovering from dipsomania, had replied, 'But I only say don't *trouble* to put milk in mine.'

'It isn't what you say, it's what you get.'

They sat later at a polished oak refectory table silently eating a suet-laden supper which represented the monastic idea at St Philumena's. Their mouths worked silently, rhythmically, chew-pause-chew-pause-swallow-pause-chew. A sister from the convent next door was reading aloud the 'holy work' prescribed for mealtimes. Caroline recognized the Epistle of St John, and listened, fixing her eyes on the white blouse of Mrs Hogg opposite. Soon her mind was on Mrs Hogg, and the recent dispute about the tea. She began to take in the woman's details: an angular face, cropped white hair, no eyelashes, rimless glasses, a small fat nose of which the tip was twitching as she ate, very thin neck, a colossal bosom. Caroline realized that she had been staring at Mrs Hogg's breasts for some time, and was aware at the same moment that the woman's nipples were showing dark and prominent through her cotton blouse. The woman was apparently wearing nothing underneath. Caroine looked swiftly away, sickened at the sight, for she was prim; her sins of the flesh had been fastidious always.

That was the first evening.

And this was the third day. At the end of the long corridor they turned. Caroline looked at her watch. Mrs Hogg did not go away.

'The Manders converted you. They are always converting somebody.'

'No. Not in my case, they didn't.'

'The Manders are *very* nice people,' said Mrs Hogg defensively.

'Charming people.'

'*Very* good people,' Mrs Hogg insisted.

'I agree,' said Caroline.

'You couldn't possibly disagree. What made you a Catholic then?'

'Many reasons,' Caroline said, 'which are not too easy to define: and so I prefer not to discuss them.'

'Mm ... I know your type,' Mrs Hogg said, 'I got your type the first evening you came. There's a lot of the Protestant about you still. You'll have to get rid of it. You're the sort that doesn't mix. Catholics are very good mixers. Why won't you talk about your conversion? Conversion's a wonderful thing. It's not *Catholic* not to talk about it.'

The woman was a funny old thing in her way. Caroline suddenly felt light-hearted. She giggled and looked again at her watch.

'I must be going.'

'Benediction isn't till three o'clock.'

'Oh, but I've come here for rest and quiet.'

'But you're not in Retreat.'

'Oh yes, you know, I *am* in retreat.' Then Caroline remembered that the popular meaning of 'retreat' in religious circles was an organized affair, not a private retiring from customary activities, so as to possess one's soul in peace. She added, 'I mean, I've retreated from London, and now I'm here for rest and quiet.'

'You were speaking plenty to that young lawyer this morning.'

In her private neurotic amusement Caroline decided to yield. Ten more minutes of Mrs Hogg. The rain pelted with sudden fury against the windows while she turned to the woman with a patronizing patience.

'Tell me about yourself, Mrs Hogg.'

Mrs Hogg had recently been appointed Catering Warden. 'If it wasn't for the Faith I couldn't hold down the job. On my feet from six till two, then on again at three and then two hours' break till supper and then there's the breakfast to think about. And I've got a great number of Crosses. That young lawyer you've got in with, the other night he said, "I don't take milk in my tea" – did you hear him? Sometimes we have as many as a hundred and thirty. Suppose a hundred and thirty people wanted tea without milk –'

'Well, that would be fairly easy,' said Caroline.

'Suppose they each wanted something different.'

'All at the same time?' said Caroline.

Seeing Mrs Hogg's expression at this moment, Caroline thought, 'Now it has struck her that I'm an enemy of the Faith.'

But Mrs Hogg righted herself; her mechanism was regulated for a chat.

'I'll tell you how I came here – it was a miracle. Our Lady sent me.'

But Caroline's mood had changed again. Her sophisticated forbearance departed and constriction took its place; a pinching irritated sense of being with something abominable, not to be tolerated. She had a sudden intense desire to clean her teeth.

'Oh tell me about the miracle,' Caroline said. Her tone was slightly menacing. 'Tell me all the details.' These scatty women with their miracles. Caroline thought, 'I hate all women and of all women Mrs Hogg. My nerves are starting up again. The next few eternal minutes are important. I must mind what I say. Keep aloof. Watch my manners at all costs.'

'Well,' Mrs Hogg was saying, 'I was of two minds whether to take a post in Bristol with a lady who was having her baby at home – I'm a registered midwife, you know, although most of my experience has been as a governess. One time I was housekeeper to a priest for two years. That was in Birmingham. He was sent to Canada in 1935, and when we said good-bye he said, "Well, Mrs Hogg –" '

'What about the miracle?' said Caroline, and to cover up her testiness overdid it and added, 'I can't hear enough about miracles.'

And, privately she consoled herself with the words, 'Little dear' – for that was how she spoke to herself on occasion – 'you will receive letters tomorrow morning from the civilized world.'

'Well, you know,' Mrs Hogg was saying, 'to *me* it was a miracle. I was debating whether to take the job in Bristol or a permanent place in the north with a deaf lady. A letter arrived, it was a Tuesday morning, to say that the lady in Bristol had gone to hospital because of some complications, and was having her baby there. The husband sent me a week's money. Then in the afternoon another letter arrived from the other place. No, I'm wrong, it was the next morning. The deaf lady had died. So there I was without a job. So I said to Our Lady, "What am I going to do now?" and Our Lady said, "Go back to St Philumena's and think it over." I'd already stayed at St Philumena's on one of the big Retreats –'

'Did you actually hear a voice?' Caroline inquired.

'A voice?'

'I mean, when you say, "Our Lady said", do you mean she spoke audibly to you?'

'Oh no. But that's how Our Lady always speaks to me. I ask a question and she answers.'

'How do you hear her answer, then?'

'The words come to me – but of course you won't know much about that. You have to be experienced in the spiritual life.'

'How do you know the words come from the Blessed Virgin?' Caroline persisted relentlessly. Mrs Hogg moved her upper lip into an indecent smile. Caroline thought:

'She desires the ecstasy of murdering me in some prolonged ritualistic orgy; she sees I am thin, angular, sharp,
inquiring; she sees I am grisly about the truth; she sees
I am well-dressed and good-looking. Perhaps she senses
my weakness, my loathing of human flesh where the bulk
outweighs the intelligence.'

Mrs Hogg continued: 'I know it was Our Lady's message because of what happened. I came to St Philumena's,
and saw Lady Manders who was here just at that time.
When I told her the position she said, "Now, there *is* a
job for you here, if you like to try it. We want to get rid
of the Catering Warden, she isn't strong enough for the
job. It's hard work, but Our Lady would help you." So I
came for a month's trial. That was in the autumn, and
I'm loving it, every minute of it.'

'That was the miracle,' Caroline said.

'Oh, it *was* a miracle. My arriving here just when Lady
Manders wanted to make a change in the staff. I only
came, really, to think things over. But I can tell you, I
don't have much chance to sit on my behind and think.
It's hard work. And I always put duty first, before everything. And I don't mind the work; Our Lady helps me.
When the kitchen girls grumble about the work, I always
tell them, "Our Lady will do it for you." And she does.'

'In that case, there's no need for them to do it,' Caroline
said.

'Now listen to me, Caroline,' said Mrs Hogg. 'You want
to speak to a priest. You haven't really got the hang of the
Catholic Faith. You want to speak to Father Ingrid.'

'You are wrong,' Caroline said. 'I've heard him speaking once from the pulpit. Once was enough. I must go
now.'

The bell was ringing for Benediction. 'That's not the
way to the chapel,' Mrs Hogg called after her as Caroline
walked swiftly along the green-walled corridors.

Caroline did not reply. She went to her room and began
to pack her things, neatly and calmly. St Philumena's was
a dead loss, Caroline told herself; 'For one who demands

35

much of life, there is always a certain amount of experience to be discarded as soon as one discovers its fruitlessness.'

She excelled at packing a suitcase. She told herself 'I'm good at packing a suitcase', forming these words in her mind to keep other words, other thoughts, from crowding in. The three days of St Philumena's were bleating to high heaven for formulation, but she kept them at bay as she muttered, 'Shoes there. Books here. The comb-bag in that corner. Blouses flat on the bed. Fold the arms. Like that. Then fold again. This way, that way. Hot-water bottle. Nothing rattling. Crucifix wedged in cotton wool. Catholic Truth Society pamphlet to read in the train. I am doing what I am doing.'

In this way, she subjugated St Philumena's for half an hour. She had devised the technique in the British Museum Reading Room almost a year ago, at a time when her brain was like a Guy Fawkes night, ideas cracking off in all directions, dark idiot-figures jumping round a fiery junk-heap in the centre.

In the train Caroline swung her case on to the rack and sat down. The case jutted out at an angle. Caroline got up and pushed it straight. She had the carriage to herself. After a while she rose again and moved the case to the middle of the rack, measuring by the mirror beneath until there was an equal space on either side. Then she sat down in her corner-seat facing it. She sat perfectly still while her thoughts became blind. Every now and then a cynical lucidity would overtake part of her mind, forcing her to comment on the fury of the other half. That was painful. She observed, 'The mocker is taking over.'

'Very funny, very funny,' said Caroline out loud. A woman just then passing in the corridor observed her talking to herself. Caroline thought, 'Good God, now my trouble is growing noticeable.'

The shock of having been observed brought some relief. As her mental pain subsided, Caroline began to reflect.

36

'Am I justified? I bloody well am.' Carefully and intently she began to recollect what St Philumena's had been like.

On her second evening when she had joined the other residents in the recreation-room, 'I must remember they are called "pilgrims",' she thought. She had already made the blunder of referring to them as 'residents'.

Anyway, there were eight of them besides Caroline. She brought them one by one to mind as she sat, still as a telegraph post, in the train which carried her to London.

That evening she had looked very seldom at her fellow guests, but now revoking, she peered into their eyes, stared up and down at their clothes, scrutinized the very skin on their faces.

She recalled them, first singly, and then in a half-circle round the fireplace; she could even see herself.

And as the train chugged south, her memory dwelling continuously on the fireside group, while at the same time she repeated mentally the formula of the rosary, touched the beads imperceptibly in her pocket, which she did for its outward effect on her person, the automatic act of the rosary prevented her from fidgeting in her agitation, it stopped her talking aloud to herself, made her unnoticeable. For the group round St Philumena's fire inflamed her; after all, she was a most jumpy woman at the best of times.

Two nights ago that group were exchanging anecdotes about the treatment of Catholics in England by non-Catholics. It was their favourite theme.

'What do you think, they won't employ Catholics on the passenger transport where my mother lives.'

'Not one Catholic child got a scholarship. . . .'

'Forty per cent were Catholics, but not one . . .'

It was well known, said a large florid lady from the West of Ireland, that the University of Cambridge would not take Catholics.

'Oh no, that's not true,' Caroline said at once.

'And they do their best for to set the Catholics asunder,' the lady from the West of Ireland went on.

'Not noticeably,' Caroline said.

The young lawyer agreed with her, but his testimony was suspect. The lady from Ireland whispered aloud to her neighbour.

'He's curing from alcohol, poor lad.'

The lawyer added, 'Of course, there's always a prejudice in certain quarters,' which put him right with the company.

'My brother in the public library, when they found he was a Catholic...'

As the atrocities mounted up, the lady from the West of Ireland continued to ply Caroline, 'What d'ye make of that? ... Isn't it awful? What d'ye think of it?'

At last, rising to leave, 'I think it very quaint,' Caroline answered.

Throughout, Mrs Hogg had been volubly present. She too had offered some relishes, had known what persecution was, and her eyes were frequently directed towards Caroline the suspect.

Recalling these proceedings, Caroline recalled too a similar fireside pattern, her family on the Jewish side with their friends, so long ago left behind her. She saw them again, nursing themselves in a half-circle as they indulged in their debauch of unreal suffering; 'Prejudice!' '... an outright insult!' Caroline thought, Catholics and Jews; the Chosen, infatuated with a tragic image of themselves. They are tragic only because they are so comical. But the thought of those fireside martyrs, Jews and Catholics, revolted Caroline with their funniness. She thought she might pull the emergency cord, halt the train, create a blinding distraction: and even while planning this action she reflected that she would not positively perform it.

But in her own rapacity for suffering, Caroline seized and held the images of the world she had left years ago and the world she had newly entered. She tugged and pulled the rosary in her pocket, while her thoughts, fine as teeth, went into action again and again with the fireside congregations of mock martyrs, their incongruity beside the real ones ... it was an insult.

It was in the dining-car that Caroline got round once more to Mrs Hogg. Mrs Hogg stuck in her mind like a lump of food on the chest which will move neither up nor down. Suddenly Caroline realized that she was bolting her lunch, and simultaneously the memory of mealtimes at St Philumena's returned, with the sight of Mrs Hogg chewing in rhythm with the reading from the Scriptures delivered in the sister's refined modulations: 'Beloved, let us love one another, love springs from God. ... If a man boasts of loving God, while he hates his own brother, he is a liar ... the man who loves God must be one who loves his brother.'

Caroline thought, 'The demands of the Christian religion are exorbitant, they are outrageous. Christians who don't realize that from the start are not faithful. They are dishonest; their teachers are talking in their sleep. "Love one another ... brethren, beloved ... your brother, neighbours, love, love, love" – do they know what they are saying?'

She had stopped eating, was conscious of two things, a splitting headache and Mrs Hogg. These bemused patterers on the theme of love, had they faced Mrs Hogg in person? Returning to her carriage Caroline passed a married couple who had been staying at St Philumena's, on their way to the dining-car. They had been among the fireside company. She remembered that they were to have left today.

'Oh, it's you, Miss Rose! I didn't think you were leaving so soon.'

People were pressing to pass, which gave Caroline a chance to escape. 'I was called away,' she said, moving off.

The couple had been received into the Church two months ago, so they had told the company round the fire. Their new-found faith was expressed in a rowdy contempt for the Church of England, in which the woman's father was a clergyman. 'Father was furious when we went over to Rome. Of course he's Anglo-Catholic; they have holy water and the saints; everything bar the Faith; too killing.' She was a large-boned and muscled woman in her mid-thirties. She had set in her final development, at the stage of athletic senior prefect. She had some hair on her face. Her lower lip had a minor pugilistic twist. Of the two, she made the more noise, but her husband, with his smooth thin face, high pink colouring, who looked as if he never needed to shave, was a good support for his wife as they sat round the fire at St Philumena's. He said, 'The wonderful thing about being a Catholic is that it makes life so easy. Everything easy for salvation and you can have a happy life. All the little things that the Protestants hate, like the statues and the medals, they all help us to have a happy life.' He finished there, as if he had filled up the required page of his school exercise book, and need state no more; he lay back in his chair, wiped his glasses, crossed his legs.

At this point the West of Ireland took over, warning them, 'Converts have a lot to learn. You can always tell a convert from a cradle Catholic. There's something different.'

The dipsomaniac lawyer, with his shiny blue suit, said, 'I like converts', and smiled weakly at Caroline. His smile faded away before Mrs Hogg's different smile.

At Crewe, Caroline got the compartment to herself again. She began to reflect that Mrs Hogg could easily become an obsession, the demon of that carnal hypocrisy which struck her mind whenever she came across a gathering of Catholics or Jews engaged in their morbid communal pleasures. She began to think of her life in London, her work, Laurence to whom she must send a wire; he would be amused by her account of St Philumena's. She began to giggle, felt drowsy, and, settling into her corner, fell asleep.

Chapter 3

WHEN Laurence returned to the cottage after posting his letter to Caroline his grandmother handed him a telegram.

He read it. 'It's from Caroline. She's back in London.'

'Yes, funny, I had a feeling it was from Caroline.' Louisa very often revealed a mild form of the gipsy's psychic faculties. 'Fancy, what a pity you've posted that letter to Liverpool.'

As Laurence set off to the post office again to telephone Caroline, he said, 'Shall I ask her to come down here?'

'Yes, certainly,' Louisa said with that inclination of her head which was a modified form of the regal gesture. When he was small she used to tell Laurence 'Don't just answer "Yes"; say "Yes, certainly", that's how Queen Mary always answers.'

'How do you know that, Grandmother?'

'A person told me.'

'Are you sure the person was telling the truth?'

'Oh yes, certainly.'

'Tell Caroline,' Louisa called after him, 'that I have some blackberries in my tins,' meaning by this to tell Laurence of her genuine desire for Caroline's visit.

'All right, I will.'

'And ask the post office to give you back the letter. There's no reason to send it all the way to Liverpool.'

'Oh, they won't fish it out without a fuss,' Laurence told her. 'They never give you back a letter, once it's posted. Not without a fuss.'

'Oh, what a pity!'

'It doesn't matter,' Laurence said. 'I'll be seeing Caroline. I wonder why she left so soon?'

'Yes, I wonder why.'

Caroline's number was engaged when he rang. The sky

41

had cleared and the autumn sun, low in the sky, touched the countryside. He decided to go to Ladle Sands, a half-hour's walk, from where he could try Caroline's number again, and by which time the pubs would be open. He was impatient to talk to Caroline. His desire to get her interested and involved in the mystery surrounding his grandmother was almost a fulfilment of a more compelling desire to assert the continuing pattern of their intimacy.

Laurence had no success with Caroline's phone that night. He pursued the exchange with mounting insistence on the urgency of getting through; they continued to reply in benumbed and fatalistic tones that the phone was out of order, it had been reported.

A queer buzzing sound brought Caroline to the telephone just before midnight. 'Your receiver has been off. We've been trying to get a call through from Sussex.' They were extremely irate.

'It hasn't been off,' said Caroline.

'It must have been misplaced. Please replace your receiver.'

'And the call? Are you putting it through?'

'No. The caller has gone now.'

Caroline thought, 'Well, he will ring in the morning.' She lay on her divan staring out at the night sky beyond her balcony, too tired to draw the curtains. She was warmed by the knowledge that Laurence was near to hand, wanting to speak to her. She could rely on him to take her side, should there be any difficulty with Helena over her rapid departure from St Philumena's. On the whole she did not think there would be any difficulty with Helena.

Just then she heard the sound of a typewriter. It seemed to come through the wall on her left. It stopped, and was immediately followed by a voice remarking her own thoughts. It said: *On the whole she did not think there would be any difficulty with Helena.*

There seemed, then, to have been more than one voice:

it was a recitative, a chanting in unison. It was something like a concurrent series of echoes. Caroline jumped up and over to the door. There was no one on the landing or on the staircase outside. She returned to her sitting-room and shut the door. Everything was quiet. The wall, from which direction the sounds had come, divided her sitting-room from the first-floor landing of a house converted into flats. Caroline's flat occupied the whole of this floor. She had felt sure the sounds had come from the direction of the landing. Now she searched the tiny flat. The opposite wall separated the bed-sitting-room from the bathroom and kitchen. Everything was quiet there. She went out on to the balcony from where she could see the whole length of Queen's Gate. Two servicemen clattered up the street and turned into Cromwell Road. The neighbouring balconies were dark and empty. Caroline returned to the room, closed the windows, and drew the curtains.

She had taken the flat four weeks ago. The house held six flats, most of which were occupied by married couples or young men who went out to their offices every day. Caroline knew the other tenants only by sight, greeting them in passing on the staircase. There were occasional noises at night, when someone had a party, but usually the house was quiet. Caroline tried to recall the tenants in the flat above hers. She was not certain; they all passed her landing on their way upstairs and she herself had never gone beyond the first floor.

A typewriter and a chorus of voices: What on earth are they up to at this time of night? Caroline wondered. But what worried her were the words they had used, coinciding so exactly with her own thoughts.

Then it began again. Tap-tappity-tap; the typewriter. And again, the voices: Caroline ran out on to the landing, for it seemed quite certain the sound came from that direction. No one was there. The chanting reached her as she returned to her room, with these words exactly:

What on earth are they up to at this time of night?

43

Caroline wondered. But what worried her were the words they had used, coinciding so exactly with her own thoughts.

And then the typewriter again: tap-tap-tap. She was rooted. 'My God!' she cried aloud. 'Am I going mad?'

As soon as she had said it, and with the sound of her own voice, her mind was filled with an imperative need to retain her sanity. It was the phrase 'Caroline wondered' which arrested her. Immediately then, shaken as she was, Caroline began to consider the possibilities, whether the sounds she had heard were real or illusory. While the thought terrified her that she was being haunted by people – spirits or things – beings who had read her thoughts, perhaps who could read her very heart, she could not hope for the horrible alternative. She feared it more; she feared that those sounds, so real that they seemed to have come from the other side of the wall, were hallucinations sent forth from her own mind. Caroline sat for the next half-hour dazed and frightened, wondering what to do. She dreaded a repetition of the experience, yet prayed for some sign that her mind was not unhinged. The question began to appear as one on which she could herself decide; it was like being faced with a choice between sanity and madness.

She had already concluded that the noise could not have come from anyone in the house. The fact that her feelings and reflections were being recorded seemed to point to some invisible source, the issue being, was it objectively real or was it imaginary? If the sounds came from some real, invisible typewriter and voices, Caroline felt she was in danger, might go mad, but the experience was not itself a sign of madness. She was now utterly convinced that what she had heard was not the product of her own imagination. 'I am not mad. I'm not mad. See; I can reflect on the situation. I am being haunted. I am not haunting myself.' Meantime, she was trembling, frightened out of her wits, although her fear was not altogether blind.

Tap-click-tap. The voices again: *Meantime, she was trembling, frightened out of her wits, although her fear was not altogether blind.*

'Christ!' she said. 'Who *is* it there?' Although she had decided quite reasonably that no one in the house could be responsible for those sounds, none the less when she actually heard the voices again, so clear, just behind the wall, she sprang up and began to search every corner of the flat, even under the divan, which was too low to conceal a human body; even in the little cupboard where the gas meter was fixed. The activity took the edge off her panic, and although she knew she would not find her tormentors in this way, she put all her energy into the search, moving furniture, opening and shutting doors. She suspected everything, however improbable; even that the sound might be contained in some quite small object – a box with a machine inside, operated from a distance. She acted upon these suspicions, examining everything closely in case she should find something strange.

There was suddenly a knocking from the ceiling. Caroline propelled herself out of the flat and switched on the landing lights.

'Who's there?' she called up the stairs. 'Who is it?' Her voice was strained high with fear.

There was a movement above her, round the bend of the stair. A shuffle, and the opening of a door on the second landing. A woman's voice whispered fiercely, 'Keep quiet!'

Looking straight above her, Caroline saw the top half of a woman leaning over the banister, long wisps of grey hair falling over her face and her loose white garment showing between the banisters. Caroline screamed, was too late to stop herself when she recognized the woman as the occupant of the flat above.

'Are you drunk?' the angry tenant breathed at her. 'What do you mean by waking the house at this time of night? It's twenty-two minutes past one, and you've been

45

banging about moving furniture and slamming doors for the last hour. I haven't slept a wink. I've got to go out to business in the morning.'

Another door opened on the second floor, and a man's voice said, 'Anything the matter? I heard a girl scream.' The woman scuttled back into her room, being undressed, and finished her complaint with her head only showing outside her door.

'It was that young woman downstairs. She's been making a disturbance for the past hour. Did you hear her?'

'I certainly heard a scream,' the man's voice said.

Caroline ran up a few steps so as to see the speakers from the bend in the staircase. 'I got a terrible fright when I saw you,' she explained to the woman. 'Was that you knocking?'

'Indeed it was,' said the woman. 'I'll complain about this in the morning.'

'Were *you* using a typewriter?' Caroline began to inquire. She was helpless and shaky. 'I heard a typewriter, and voices.'

'You're mad!' said the woman, as she withdrew and shut the door. The young man had also retreated.

Caroline returned to her rooms, and, rapidly and stealthily, began to pack a small suitcase. She wondered where she would spend the rest of the night. A lonely hotel room was unthinkable, it would have to be a friend's house. She moved about, jerkily snatching at the necessary articles as if she expected some invisible hand, concealed in each object, to close over hers before she had got possession of it. She was anxious to make as little sound as possible, but in her nervousness bumped into the furniture and knocked over a glass dish. To protect herself from the noises of her movements, she contracted a muscle somewhere behind her nose and throat, which produced the effect in her ears as of a rustling breeze – it dulled the sound of her footsteps, making the whole operation sound quieter than it was.

Caroline pressed down the lid of her small case. She had decided where to go for the night. The Baron; he was awake, or at least available, at all hours. She opened the case again, remembering that she had packed her money; she would need it for the taxi to the Baron's flat in Hampstead. She was absorbed by the pressing need to get out of her flat at the earliest possible moment, and as she searched among her clothes she did not even notice, with her customary habit of self-observation, that she had thrown her night-things together anyhow. The difference between this frenzied packing operation and the deliberate care she had taken, in spite of her rage, to fold and fit her possessions into place at St Philumena's less than a day ago failed to register.

Tap-tick-tap. Tap. She did not even notice Click-tappity with her customary habit of self-observation, that she had thrown her night-things together anyhow. The difference between this frenzied packing operation and the deliberate care she had taken, in spite of her rage, to fold and fit her possessions into place at St Philumena's less than a day ago failed to register. Tap.

Coat – hat – handbag – suitcase; Caroline grabbed them and hustled out of the door, slamming it to. She rattled downstairs and out of the front door, which she slammed behind her. At the top of Queen's Gate, turning in from Old Brompton Road, she got a taxi and secured herself inside it with a slam of the door.

'It is quite a common thing,' Willi Stock said. 'Your brain is overworked.' This was the Baron speaking. He stood by the electric fire with its flicking imitation coals, sipping Curaçao.

Caroline sipped hers, curled up on the sofa, and crying. Absorbing the warmth of the fire and of the liquor, she felt a warmth of gratitude towards the Baron. For the last hour he had been explaining her mental condition. She was consoled, not by the explanations, but by the fact of his recognizable face, by the familiar limitations of his mind, and by the reality of his warm flat and his bottle of Curaçao.

For the first time in her life, she felt that Willi Stock was an old friend. Regarding him in this category, she was able to secure her conscience in his company. For the Baron belonged to one of the half-worlds of Caroline's past, of which she had gradually taken leave; it was a society which she had half-forgotten, and of which she had come wholly to disapprove. It was over a year since she had last seen the Baron. But Laurence had kept up with him, had mentioned him from time to time, which confirmed Caroline in her feeling that she was in the company of an old friend. She greatly needed the protection of an old friend till daylight.

He said, 'Eleanor is away on tour just now.'

Caroline said, 'I know, Laurence had a postcard.'

Eleanor Hogarth was the Baron's mistress.

'Did he?' said the Baron. 'When was that?'

'Oh, last week sometime. He merely mentioned it.'

They called him the Baron because he called himself Baron Stock. Caroline was not aware from what aristocracy he derived his title: nor had anyone inquired; she was sure it was not self-imposed as some suggested. He came originally from the Belgian Congo, had travelled in the Near East, loitered in Europe, and finally settled in England, a naturalized British subject. That was fifteen years ago, and he was now nearing fifty. Caroline had always felt that the Baron had native African blood, without being able to locate its traces in any one feature. She had been in Africa, and had a sense of these things. It was a matter of casual curiosity to her; but she had noticed, some years ago, when Africa's racial problems were being discussed in company with the Baron, he had denounced the blacks with ferocious bitterness, out of all proportion to the occasion. This confirmed Caroline's judgement; there was, too, an expression of pathos which at times appeared on the Baron's face, which she had seen in others of concealed mixed colour; and there was some-

48

thing about the whites of his eyes; what it was she did not know. And altogether, having observed these things, she did not much care.

The Baron had set up a bookshop in Charing Cross Road, one of those which keep themselves exclusively intellectual. 'Intellect-u-al,' the Baron pronounced it. He would say, 'Of course there are no intellect-u-als in England.'

It had been the delight of Caroline and Laurence to recall the day when they looked in on the Baron at Charing Cross Road, to find him being accosted by a tiny woman with the request:

'D'you have any railway books for children?'

The Baron reared high and thin on the central expanse of grey carpet and regarded her silently for half a second.

'Railway books for children,' she repeated. 'Books with pictures of trains and railways.'

The Baron said: 'Railway books for children, Madam? I do not think so, Madam.' His arm languidly indicated the shelves. 'We have Histor-ay, Biograph-ay, Theolog-ay, Theosoph-ay, Psycholog-ay, Religio-n, Poetr-ay, but railway books for children. ... Try Foyles across the road, Madam.'

He raised his shoulders and eyebrows as he turned to Laurence and Caroline. 'My father,' he said, 'knew a man in the Belgian Diplomatic Service who was the author of a railway book for children. It was very popular and sold quickly. A copy was sent to a family in Yugoslavia. Of course, the book contained a code message. The author was revising the book for the second edition when he was arrested. That story is my total experience of railway books for children. Have you read this work on Kafka? – it has just come in, my darlings, my Laurence and my Caroline.'

In this way, Baron Stock was an old friend.

Caroline lay in the dark warm room on a made-up sofa bed. The Baron had left her just after four had struck.

49

She had stopped crying. In case she should want them, the Baron had left a bottle of aspirins on a chair by the sofa. Caroline reached out for the bottle, unscrewed the cap and extracted the twist of cotton wool which she had hoped to find. She stuffed a piece in each ear. Now she was alone, it seemed to her that she had been playing a false role with the Baron. It was the inevitable consequence of her arrival at his flat in a panic, at a late hour; 'Willi! Let me in, I've been hearing voices!'

After that, she was forced to accept his protection, his friendliness; was glad of it. And when he had settled her by the fire:

'Caroline, *my* dear, how slender and febrile you've become! What kind of voices? How extremely interesting. Was it a religi-ous experience?'

She had begun to weep, to apologize.

'Caroline, *my* dear, as you know, I never go to bed. Seriously, I never go to bed unless it's the last possible alternative. I am delighted beyond words – Caroline, my dear, I am so honoured – your distress, my dear – if you can realize how I feel.'

And so she had to play the part. Now, alone in the dark, she thought, 'I should have faced it out at the flat. I shouldn't have run away.'

The Baron, of course, was convinced she was suffering from a delusion.

'It happens to many many people, my dear. It is quite nothing to worry about. If the experience should recur you will have a course of analysis or take some pills and the voices will go away. But I doubt that the phenomenon will recur. You have been under a considerable strain from what I hear of your severed relations with Laurence.'

'We haven't parted, really, you know.'

'But you now have separate establishments?'

'Yes, I've got rooms in Kensington. Laurence is keeping on the flat for the time being. He's away in the country. I must get in touch with him tomorrow, first thing.'

She gave the deliberate impression of not wanting to talk any more.

'In Sussex? With Mrs Jepp?' – a genuine curiosity in his voice.

'Yes.'

'I met her one day about three years ago. Laurence introduced me. A fine old lady. Wonderful for her age. Quite excellent. Do you see much of her?'

'I saw her last Easter,' Caroline said, 'she was grand.'

'Yes, she is grand. She doesn't visit London, of course?'

'No,' Caroline said. 'That must have been her last trip when you met her. She hasn't been to London since.'

'She doesn't care for the Hampstead ménage?'

'Well, she's an independent soul,' said Caroline absently.

She had only half taken in the Baron's chatter, although he continued to speak of Louisa.

'I must get in touch with Laurence first thing,' Caroline repeated. 'Mrs Jepp isn't on the phone. I'll send a wire. Oh, Willi! – those voices, it was Hell!'

Now, lying awake in the dark, Caroline recalled the conversation, regretting that she had shown such a supine dependence on the Baron. More and more she thought, 'I should have stayed at home and faced whatever was to be faced.' She knew she had tough resources. And as she tormented herself, now, into confronting her weakness, painfully she recollected the past hour; some of the talk which she had let slip so drowsily through her mind came back to her. It had struck her in passing that the Baron had seemed extraordinarily interested in Laurence's grandmother. He was the last person one would expect to have remembered – and by name – an undistinguished old lady to whom he had been introduced casually three years ago. Mrs Jepp was not immediately impressive to strangers, was not at all the type to impress the Baron.

Through the darkness, from beside the fireplace, Caroline heard a sound. *Tap*. The typewriter. She sat up as the voices followed:

The Baron had seemed extraordinarily interested in Laurence's grandmother. He was the last person one would expect to have remembered – and by name – an undistinguished old lady to whom he had been introduced casually three years ago. Mrs Jepp was not immediately impressive to strangers.

Caroline yelled, 'Willi! Oh, my God, the voices. ... Willi!'

Through the wall she heard him stir.

'Did you call, Caroline?'

Eventually he shuffled in and switched on the light.

Caroline pulled the bulky borrowed dressing-gown over her shoulders, her eyes blue and hard with fright. She had grasped the rosary which she had tucked under the cushion at her head. Her fingers clung shakily to the beads as a child clings to its abracadabra toy.

'*My* dear Caroline, what a charming picture you make! Don't move for a second, don't move: I am trying to recall – some moment, some scene in the past or a forgotten canvas – One of my sister's friends perhaps – or my nurse. Caroline, my dear, there is no more exquisite sight than that of a woman taken unawares with a rosary.'

Caroline slung the beads on the post of the chair. The thought flashed upon her, 'He is indecent.' She looked up at him sharply and caught him off his guard; his mouth and eyes drooped deadly tired, and he was resisting a yawn. She thought, 'After all, he is kind; it was only a pose.'

'Tell me about the voices,' he said. 'I heard nothing, myself. From what direction did they come?'

'Over there, beside the fireplace,' she answered.

'Would you like some tea? I think there is tea.'

'Oh, coffee. Could I have some coffee? I don't think I'm likely to sleep.'

'We shall both have some coffee. Stay where you are.'

Caroline thought, 'He means that he isn't likely to sleep, either.' She said, 'I'm awfully sorry about this,

52

Willi. It sounds so foolish, but it really is appalling. And you must be dead tired.'

'Coffee and aspirins. *My* Caroline, you are not to apologize, I am delighted –'

But he could hardly conceal his sleepiness. As he returned bearing their coffee, with a bottle of brandy on a tray, he said, as one who keeps the conversation flowing, notwithstanding a tiger in the garden, 'You must tell me all about the voices.' He saw her removing the cotton-wool plugs from her ears, but pretended not to notice. 'I have always believed that disembodied beings inhabit this room,' he went on, 'and now I'm sure. Seriously, I'm sure – indissuasibly convinced, Caroline, that you are in touch with something. I do so wish I had been able to give you some phenobarbitone, an excellent sedative; or something to make you sleep. But of course I shall sit up with you, it's nearly five already. . . .'

He said no more about hallucinations, by which Caroline understood that he now really believed that she was crazy. She sipped her coffee submissively and jerkily, weeping all the time. She told him to leave her.

'Of course not. I want to hear about the voices. It's most intriguing, really.'

She felt better for the effort to describe what had happened, although the fact gnawed at her that the Baron was finding the episode a strain and a nuisance. But ruthlessly, in her own interest, she talked on and on. And as she talked she realized that the Baron was making the best of it, had resigned himself, was attending to her, but as one who regards another's words, not as symbols but as symptoms.

He got out of her that the clicking of the typewriter always preceded the voices, and sometimes accompanied their speech. How many voices there were, she could not say. Male or female? Both, she told him. It was impossible to disconnect the separate voices, because they came in complete concert; only by the varying timbres could the chorus be distinguished from one voice. 'In fact,' she went on, wound-up and talking rapidly, 'it sounds like one person speaking in several tones at once.'

'And always using the past tense?'

'Yes. Mocking voices.'

'And you say this chorus comments on your thoughts and actions?'

'Not always,' said Caroline, 'that's the strange thing. It says "Caroline was thinking or doing this or that" – then sometimes it adds a remark of its own.'

'Give me an example, dear. I'm so stupid – I can never grasp –'

'Well,' said Caroline, unwhelming herself of a sudden access of confidence in the Baron's disinterestedness, 'take tonight. I was dropping off, and thinking over my con-versation with you –

'– as one does –' she added,

'– and it drifted to my mind how you had remembered meeting Laurence's grandmother; I thought it strange you should do so. Next thing, I heard the typewriter and the voices. They repeated my thought, something like, "It came to her that the Baron" – you know we always call you the Baron, "– that the Baron had been extraordinarily interested in Laurence's grandmother." That's what the voices said. And then they added something to the effect that the Baron was the last person who would remember, and remember by name, an old woman like Mrs Jepp merely from a passing introduction three years ago. You see, Willi, the words are immaterial –'

'You're mad,' said the Baron abruptly.

Caroline felt relieved at these words, although, and in a way because, they confirmed her distress. It was a relief to hear the Baron speak his true mind, it gave her exactly what she had anticipated, what seemed to her a normal person's reaction to her story. Fearing this, she had been purposely vague when, earlier in the evening, she had explained her distress: 'A typewriter followed by voices. They speak in the past tense. They mock me.'

Now that she had been more explicit, and had been told

54

she was mad, she felt a perverse satisfaction at the same time as a suffocating sense that she might never communicate the reality of what she had heard.

The Baron hastily recovered. 'I use "mad" of course in the colloquial sense. In the way that we're *all mad*, you know. A little crazy, you know. Amongst ourselves, I mean – the intelligentsia are all a little mad and, my dear Caroline, that's what makes us so nice. The sane are not worth noticing.'

'Oh, quite,' said Caroline. 'I know what you mean.' But she was wondering, now, why he had spoken so viciously: 'You're mad!' – like a dog snapping at a fly. She felt she had been tactless. She wished she had chosen to cite a different example of the voices.

'Someone is haunting me, that's what it is,' Caroline said, hoping to discard responsibility for offending the Baron.

He seemed to have forgotten his role as the intrigued questioner; his air of disinterested curiosity was suspended while he told Caroline exactly why and how Mrs Jepp had impressed him. 'You see, she is a charac-ter. So small and yet her strength – her aged yet vivid face. So dark, so small. I could never forget that face.'

With surprise, Caroline thought, 'He is defending himself.'

'And she looked so debonair, my dear, in a deep blue velvet hat. Her brown wrinkles. Quite a picture.'

'Three years ago, was it, Willi?'

'Almost three years – I remember it well. Laurence brought her into the shop, and she said, "What a lot of books!"'

He gave an affectionate chuckle, but Caroline did not join him. She was thinking of Louisa Jepp's last visit to London, three years ago. Certainly, she did not possess her blue hat at that time, Caroline was acquainted with all Louisa's hats. They were purchased at long intervals, on rare occasions. And only last Easter, Caroline had accompanied the old lady to Hayward's Heath where they had spent the afternoon, eventually deciding on that blue velvet hat which had so pleased Louisa that she had worn it on every occasion since.

'A blue hat?' said Caroline.

'My dear, believe it or not, a blue. I recall it distinctly. Blue velvet, curling close to her head, with a fluffy black feather at the side. I shall never forget that hat nor the face beneath it.'

That was the hat all right.

In the face of the Baron's apparent lie – to what purpose? – and the obvious fact that her account of the voices had somehow provoked it, Caroline began to gather her own strength. The glimmering of a puzzle distinct from her own problem was a merciful antidote to her bewilderment. She kept her peace and sipped her coffee, knowing that she was delivered at least from this second mockery, the Baron posing as a credulous sympathizer, his maddening chatter about psychic phenomena, while in reality he waited for the morning, when he could hand her over to Laurence or someone responsible. The Baron might think her mentally unhinged, but by a mercy she had made it clear, though quite unintentionally, that her condition was dangerous for him. In fact, she had forced him to take her seriously, to the extent that he made excuses for himself and lied.

She considered this, but when she looked at him, saw him still courteous in his extreme tiredness, her tears returned.

'Oh, Willi! How can I ever thank you? You are so kind.'

'So kind,' she repeated, she herself like a tired infant whose tongue cannot extricate itself from a single phrase, 'So kind, so kind –' And so, in her gratitude, she gave away what advantage she had gained and became once more a distracted woman seeking the protection of an old friend.

The Baron, as if he too would make a concession, and anxious to place her in a less pathetic light, asked,

'What are you writing these days?'

'Oh, the same book. But I haven't done much lately.'

'The work on the twentieth-century novel?'

'That's right. *Form in the Modern Novel.*'

'How's it going so far?'

'Not bad. I'm having difficulty with the chapter on realism.'

Suddenly she felt furious with the voices for having upset her arrangements. She had planned to start work that week; to put all her personal troubles out of her mind. And now, this ghastly humiliating experience.

She broke down again. 'It ought not to have happened to me! This sort of thing shouldn't happen to an intelligent woman!'

'It is precisely to the intelligent that these things happen,' said the Baron. Both he and Caroline were drinking brandy neat.

After a while the Baron made more coffee, and then, thank God, it was dawn.

The Baron had put up a protest, but eventually he had let her leave his flat. By daylight she had revived, with that unaccountable energy to which nervous people have access, not only in spite of a sleepless and harrowing night, but almost because of it. The Baron had put up a protest but he had let her go after she had promised to keep in touch with him during the day. She wanted to be out of his flat. She wanted to return to Kensington. And to contact Laurence; he would return to London. She would have to face the housekeeper at her flat; she was sure the other tenants must have complained of the last night's turmoil. 'The housekeeper is a brute, Willi,' Caroline had said, as she collected her things.

'Give her ten shill-ings,' said the Baron.

'It's a man.'

'Give him two pounds.'

'Perhaps a pound,' said Caroline. 'Well, Willi, I do thank you.'

'Two pounds would be on the safe side,' pursued the Baron.

'I'll make it thirty shillings,' said Caroline, seriously.

The Baron began to giggle quietly. Then Caroline, thinking it over, was taken with laughter too.

'I like to haggle.'

'All women do.'

On the way to Hampstead Underground, she sent Laurence a wire. 'Come immediately something mysterious going on.'

'The voices may never come back,' she thought. In a way she hoped they would. Laurence might easily be the means of tracking them down by some sheer innocent remark. That was the sort of thing he could do. She did not think the voices would speak to her if she was with anyone else. But Laurence would investigate. She had almost a sense of adventure in her unnatural exhilaration. It was a sharp sunny day. In the train, she put a pound note and a ten-shilling note in a separate place in her handbag, and smiled; that was for the housekeeper. On the whole, she hoped the voices would return, would give her a chance to establish their existence, and to trace their source.

It was nearly nine-thirty when she reached Queen's Gate. A convenient time. The tenants had left for their offices, and the housekeeper had not yet emerged. She closed the door quietly and crept upstairs.

Laurence kept the door of the telephone box open to let in the sun and air of the autumn morning.

'Still no reply?'

'Sorry, no reply.'

'Sure you've got the right –?'

But the operator had switched off. He was sure she hadn't got the right number – at least – maybe – Caroline must have gone somewhere else for the night. Perhaps she had gone to Mass.

He rang his parents' home. There had been no word

from Miss Rose. His mother was at Mass. His father had just left. He sent Caroline a wire from the village post office, and went for an exasperated walk, which turned cheerful as he anticipated Caroline's coming to stay at his grandmother's. He had arranged to prolong his holiday for another week. When he reached the cottage half an hour later, he found a wire from Caroline.

'There's been a mix-up at the post office,' he told Louisa.

'What, dear?'

'I sent Caroline a wire, and apparently Caroline has sent one to me. But they must have got the messages mixed up somehow. This is the message I sent to Caroline. The very words.'

'What dear? Read it out, I don't understand.'

'I'll go and speak to the post office,' Laurence said swiftly, leaving at once. He was anxious to avoid the appearance of concealing the wire from his grandmother, after admitting that it contained his own message. He read it again. 'Come immediately something mysterious going on.' It ended, 'love Caroline'.

At the post office, where a number of Louisa's neighbours were buying tea and other things, Laurence caused a slight stir. His outgoing message was compared with the one he had just received. He distinctly overheard the postmaster, in their little back office, say to his daughter, 'They've both used the exact same words. It's a code, or something fishy they've arranged beforehand.'

He came out and said to Laurence, 'The two telegrams are identical, sir.'

'Well, that's funny,' Laurence repeated the words, 'something mysterious going on'.

'Yes, it seems so,' said the man.

Laurence cleared off before the question could become more confused and public. He went into the phone box and asked for Caroline's number. It was ringing through. Immediately she answered.

'Caroline?'

'Laurence, is that you? Oh, I've just come home and found a wire. Did you send a wire?'

'Yes, did you?'

'Yes, how was it supposed to read? I'm so frightened.'

The little parlour in the Benedictine Priory smelt strongly of polish; the four chairs, the table, the floors, the window-frame gleamed in repose of the polish, as if these wooden things themselves had done some hard industry that day before dawn. Outside, the late October evening sun lit up the front garden strip, and Caroline while she waited in the parlour could hear the familiar incidence of birds and footsteps from the suburban street. She knew this parlour well, with its polish; she had come here weekly for three months to receive her instruction for the Church. She watched a fly alight on the table for a moment; it seemed to Caroline to be in a highly dangerous predicament, as if it might break through the glossy surface on which it skated. But it made off quite easily. Caroline jogged round nervily as the door opened. Then she rose as the priest came in, her friend, ageing Father Jerome. She had known him for so many years that she could not remember their first meeting. They had been in touch and out of touch for long periods. And when, after she had decided to enter the Church, and she went weekly to his Priory, her friends had said,

'Why do you go so far out of London for instruction? Why don't you go to Farm Street?' Caroline replied,

'Well, I know this priest.'

And if they were Catholics, her friends would say,

'Oh, it doesn't matter about the particular priest. The nearest priest is always the best one.'

And Caroline replied, 'Well, I know this priest.'

She wondered, now, if she did know him. He was, as usual, smiling with his russet face, limping with his bad leg, carrying a faded folder from which emerged an untidy sheaf of crumpled papers. 'I got two days off last week to copy parts of Lydgate's *Life of Our Lady* at the British

60

Museum. I've got it here. Do you know it? I'll read you a bit presently. Glorious. What are you writing? You look tired, are you sleeping well? Are you eating proper food? What did you have for breakfast?'

'I haven't slept properly for a week,' said Caroline. Then she told him about the voices.

'This started after you got back from St Philumena's?'

'Yes. That's a week ago today. And it's been going on ever since. It happens when I'm alone during the day. Laurence came up from the country. He's moved into my flat. I can't bear to be alone at nights.'

'Sleeping there?'

'In the other room,' said Caroline. 'That's all right, isn't it?'

'For the time being,' said the priest absently.

He rose abruptly and went out. The thoughts shot through Caroline's brain, 'Perhaps he's gone to fetch another priest; he thinks I'm dangerous. Has he gone to fetch a doctor? He thinks I should be certified, taken away.' And she knew those thoughts were foolish, for Father Jerome had a habit of leaving rooms abruptly when he remembered something which had to be done elsewhere. He would be back presently.

He returned very soon and sat down without comment. He was followed almost immediately by a lay brother, bearing a tray with a glass of milk and a plate of biscuits which he placed before her. This brought back to her the familiarity of the monk and the parlour; only last winter in the early dark evenings after they had finished the catechism, Father Jerome would fetch Caroline the big editions of the Christian Fathers from the monastery library, for she had loved to rummage through them. Then, when he had left her in the warm parlour turning the pages and writing out her notes, he had used to send the lay brother to her with a glass of milk and biscuits.

Now, while she sipped the milk, Father Jerome read aloud a part of *The Life of Our Lady*. He had already started putting it into modern English, and consulted

61

her on one or two points. Caroline felt her old sense of ease with the priest; he never treated her as someone far different from what she was. He treated her not only as a child; not only as an intellectual; not only as a nervy woman; not only as weird; he seemed to assume simply that she was as she was. When he asked, she told him more clearly about the voices.

'I think,' she said, 'that they are really different tones of one voice. I think they belong to one person.'

She also said, 'I think I am possessed.'

'No,' he said, 'you are not possessed. You may be obsessed, but I doubt it.'

Caroline said, 'Do you think this is a delusion?'

'How should I know?'

'Do you think I'm mad?'

'No. But you're ill.'

'That's true. D'you think I'm a neurotic?'

'Of course. That goes without saying.'

Caroline laughed too. There was a time when she could call herself a neurotic without a sense of premonition; a time when it was merely the badge of her tribe.

'If I'm not mad,' she said, 'I soon will be, if this goes on much longer.'

'Neurotics never go mad,' he said.

'But this is intolerable.'

'Doesn't it depend on how you take it?'

'Father,' she said, almost as if speaking to herself to clarify her mind, 'if only I knew where the voices came from. I think it is one person. It uses a typewriter. It uses the past tense. It's exactly as if someone were watching me closely, able to read my thoughts; it's as if the person was waiting to pounce on some insignificant thought or action, in order to make it signify in a strange distorted way. And how does it know about Laurence and my friends? And then there was a strange coincidence the other day. Laurence and I sent each other a wire with exactly the same words, at the same time. It was horrifying. Like predestination.'

'These things can happen,' said Father Jerome. 'Coincidence or some kind of telepathy.'

'But the typewriter and the voices – it is as if a writer on another plane of existence was writing a story about us.' As soon as she had said these words, Caroline knew that she had hit on the truth. After that she said no more to him on the subject.

As she was leaving he asked her how she had liked St Philumena's.

'Awful,' she said, 'I only stayed three days.'

'Well,' he said, 'I didn't think it was your sort of place. You should have gone to a Benedictine convent. They are more your sort.'

'But it was you recommended St Philumena's! Don't you remember, that afternoon at Lady Manders', you were both so keen on my going there?'

'Oh sorry. Yes, I suppose we were. What didn't you like?'

'The people.'

He chuckled. 'Yes, the people. It's a matter of how you take them.'

'I believe it is,' said Caroline as though she had just thought of something.

'Well, God bless you. Get some sleep and keep in touch.'

She found Laurence in when she returned to the flat in Queen's Gate. He was fiddling about with a black box-like object which at first she took to be a large typewriter.

'What's that?' she said, when she saw it closer.

'Listen,' said Laurence.

He pressed a key. There was a whirring sound and the box began to talk with a male voice pitched on a peculiarly forced husky note. It said, 'Caroline darling, I have a suggestion to make.' Then it went on to say something funny but unprintable.

Caroline subsided with laughter and relief on to the divan.

Laurence did something to the instrument and the words rumbled forth again.

'I knew your voice right away,' Caroline said.

'I bet you didn't. I disguised it admirably. Listen again.'

'No!' said Caroline. 'Someone might overhear it. Dirty beast you are.'

He replayed the record and they both laughed helplessly.

'What have you brought that thing here for?' Caroline said. 'It might have given me a dreadful fright.'

'To record your spook-voices. Now see. I'm placing this disc in here. If you hear them again, you press that. Then it records any voice within hearing distance.'

He had placed it against the wall where the voices came from.

'Afterwards,' he explained, 'we can take out the disc and play it back.'

'Maybe those voices won't record,' Caroline said.

'They will if they're in the air. Any sound causes an occurrence. If the sound has objective existence it will be recorded.'

'This sound might have another sort of existence and still be real.'

'Well, let's first exhaust the possibilities of the natural order –'

'But we don't know all the possibilities of the natural order.'

'If the sound doesn't record, we can take it for granted that it either doesn't exist, or it exists in some supernatural order,' he explained.

She insisted, 'It does exist. I think it's a natural sound. I don't think that machine will record it.'

'Don't you want to try it?' He seemed disappointed almost.

'Of course. It's a lovely idea.'

'And better,' he said, 'than any ideas you've had so far.'

'I've got a good one now,' Caroline said. 'I'm sure it's

the right one. It came to me while I was talking to Father Jerome.'

'Let's have it,' he said.

'Not yet. I want to assemble the evidence.'

Caroline was happy. Laurence looked at himself in the mirror, smiled, and told himself, 'She says I'm a dirty beast.'

The flat was untidy. Caroline loved to see her own arrangement of things upset by Laurence. It was a double habitation now. They had told the housekeeper that they had got married. He was only half satisfied with the story, but he would put the other half on the bill, Laurence predicted. She was used to being called 'Mrs Manders': it was easy, as if they had never parted, except for the knowledge that this was an emergency set-up. Another week, at the most, and then something would have to be done. She regretted having disclosed her plight to the Baron. He had been pressing Laurence to get Caroline into a nursing home. She did not mind this suggestion, so much as the implication. 'A nursing home.' He meant a refined looney-bin. Laurence opposed it; he wanted to take her back with him to his grandmother. The Baron had carried the story to Helena, who offered to pay Caroline's expenses at a private nursing home for Catholics. Helena did not mean a looney-bin, however.

'I wouldn't mind a few weeks' rest in a nursing home,' Caroline had told Laurence. 'I don't think they could do away with the voices, but they might deafen me to them for a while. It would be a rest.'

Laurence had been altogether against this.

And he had a mystery of his own to solve. 'I wrote and told you all about it. I'd just posted a letter to St Philumena's when I got your first wire to say you'd returned to London. I daresay it will be forwarded.'

'Do tell me.' Caroline had half-expected to hear of a 'mystery' similar to her own.

'Well, the thing is, Grandmother is mixed up with some

highly suspect parties. At first I thought she was running a gang, but now, all things considered, I think she may be their stooge.'

'No,' said Caroline. 'Quite definitely, your grandmother isn't anyone's stooge.'

'Now, d'you think that, honestly? — That's what I feel myself really. You must come and see for yourself.'

'I'll think about it,' Caroline had said.

Four times during the past week, while Laurence had been out, she had heard the typewriter and the voices.

Then she had told Laurence. 'I'll see Father Jerome. If he advises a nursing home, it's a nursing home. If he says go to your grandmother's, I'll come. I could always go into a nursing home later on.'

But she had forgotten to put these alternatives to Father Jerome. And now, she did not feel it mattered.

'I'll come to Sussex,' she said.

'Really, will you? Is that what the holy pa advised?'

'No. I forgot to mention it. He advised food and sleep.'

Laurence knew Caroline's nervous responses to food and sleep at the best of times. But she didn't laugh with him. Instead, she said, 'I feel better. I think the worst of my trouble is over; I begin to see daylight.'

He was used to Caroline's rapid recoveries, but only from physical illness. In past years, he had known her prostrated by the chest complications to which she was subject; bronchitis, pleurisy, pneumonia. Once or twice she had lain for several days, running a temperature, burning with fever. Then, overnight or in the course of an hour in the afternoon, or waking in the late morning after a kindling night, there would come a swift alteration, a lightning revival of her sick body; Caroline would say, 'I am better. I feel quite well.' She would sit up and talk. Her temperature would drop to normal. It was almost as though she was under a decision, as if her body, at such times, were only awaiting her word, and she herself submissively waiting for some secret go-ahead within her, permitting her at last to say, 'I am better. I feel well.' After

66

such rapid reversals Caroline would feel depressed, would crave that attention due to an invalid which she had not cared about in her real danger. Frequently in the days that followed, she would say, 'I'm not better yet. I'm still weak.' But there was never any conviction in this. It became a joke eventually, for Laurence to say for months after her illnesses, 'You're still an invalid. You're not better yet', and Caroline, too, would tell him, 'You make breakfast today, dear. I'm still an invalid. I'm feeling *very unwell.*'

Laurence thought of these things when he heard Caroline, on her return from the Priory, tell him, 'I feel better. ... I begin to see daylight.' He recognized this signal; he himself had nursed her through her illnesses over the past six years. Those were mostly times of poverty before his parents had accepted his irregular life with Caroline; before he got his job on the B.B.C.; before Caroline had got her literary reputation.

Caroline knew what he was thinking. He had not expected her to recover so abruptly from this sort of illness. He had seen it coming on for the past six months.

And now he was thinking – 'So she is better. She sees daylight. Is it just like that? Can she be right? No more melancholia. No more panic at the prospect of meeting strangers. No worry, no voices? Only the formal convalescence, the "invalid" period, and then the old Caroline again. Can it be so?'

Caroline saw on his face an expression which she remembered having seen before. It was a look of stumped surprise, the look of one who faces an altogether and irrational new experience; a look partly fearful, partly indignant, partly curious, but predominantly joyful. The other occasion on which she had seen this expression on Laurence's face was during an argument, when she told him of her decision to enter the Church, with the consequence that they must part. They were both distressed; they hardly knew what they were saying. In reply to some remark of Laurence she had rapped out, nastily, 'I love

God better than you!' It was then she saw on his face that mixture of surprise and dismay, somehow revealing in its midst an unconscious alien delight, which she witnessed now once more when she told him, 'The worst is over. I see daylight.'

'But remember I'm still an invalid,' she added. He laughed quite a lot. She was sorry to have to disappoint him. She knew he would be expecting her 'recovery' to be something different from what it was going to be, and that he was wondering, 'How does she know she won't hear those voices again?'

He said, 'Do you really feel that everything's going to be all right now, darling?'

'Yes,' she said. 'I'm perfectly O.K. Only a bit tired, but now, you see, I know what the voices are. It's a creepy experience but I can cope with it. I'm sure I've discovered the true cause. I have a plan. I'll tell you something about it by and by.'

She lay on the divan and closed her eyes.

'I'm worried about you,' he said.

'You mean, the voices. You mean I can't be well if I go on hearing them.'

He thought for a moment. 'Let's see if this machine records anything.'

'All right,' said Caroline. 'But supposing it doesn't, what difference does that make?'

'Well, in that case, I think you should try to understand the experience in a symbolic light.'

'But the voices are voices. Of course they are symbols. But they are also voices. There's the typewriter too – that's a symbol, but it *is* a real typewriter. I hear it.'

'My Caroline,' he said, 'I hope you will hear it no more.'

'I don't,' Caroline said.

'Don't you? Now, why?'

'Because now I know what they are. I'm on the alert now,' Caroline said. 'You see, I really am quite better. Only tired.' She raised her voice a little, and said, 'And if anyone's listening, let them take note.'

Well, well!

'I bet they feel scared,' said Laurence quite merrily.

She slipped off her skirt, and slid between the sheets of the divan.

He thought, 'And yet, she does look better. Almost well again, only tired.'

She was dozing off when he left her; he had to run over to Hampstead to see his mother; she had telephoned to him rather urgently. He promised Caroline to be back in time to take her out to dinner. Before he went he reminded her of the tape-recorder.

'Don't forget to press that lever if anything should happen,' he said. 'Sure you'll be all right?'

'Perfectly O.K.,' said Caroline drowsily. 'I could sleep for a fortnight.'

'Good. Sleep well. And if you want anything, you know, just ring my mother. I'll be over there myself in about twenty minutes.'

Caroline was very quickly asleep. And even as she slept, she felt herself appreciating her sleep; told herself, this was the best sleep she had had for six months. She told herself to sleep on, for she would wake up presently, and then she would mean business.

At this point in the narrative, it might be as well to state that the characters in this novel are all fictitious, and do not refer to any living persons whatsoever.

Tap-tappity-tap. At this point in the narrative ... Caroline sprang up and pressed the lever on the dictaphone. Then she snatched the notebook and pencil which she had placed ready, and took down in shorthand the paragraph above; she did not start to tremble until after the chanting chorus had ended. She lay trembling in the darkening room, and considered the new form of her suffering, now that she was well again and committed to health.

Chapter 4

THERE were chrysanthemums and asters in the bowls, chrysanthemums and asters almost discernible on the faded loose upholstery in the drawing-room. They needed to be replaced, but Helena Manders had never replaced them, in order that the Knighthood, which had occurred when the covers were already past their best, should make no difference. The Manders put up with many discomforts so that the Knighthood should make no difference. The fire was lit because of Laurence coming. No fires till November, as a rule.

'Are you in a hurry?' Helena said, because now Laurence had arrived and was looking at his watch. He did this because he knew that when his mother wanted to see him about any particular business, she would usually forget the business until he was ready to go, causing him to stay for dinner or to stay the night; or she would forget the business until after he had gone, in which case she would ring him again and he would have to go again.

Laurence did not mind visiting his parents at Hampstead, he even enjoyed going there to stay for meals, or for days and weeks; only this had to be in his own time, when the time was ripe, when the time came round for him to say to himself, 'I would like to go over to Hampstead.' When he was summoned there, he couldn't be bothered greatly.

And so he looked at his watch. He said, 'I've only got an hour. I'm dining with Caroline. I would have brought her, only she's resting.'

'How is Caroline?'

'She says she's better. I think she is, really.'

'Do you? And the hallucinations, have they disappeared? Poor girl, she wouldn't tell me much.'

'I don't know,' said Laurence. 'I don't know if she's better. She says she feels better.'

'Not going into a nursing home? That would be best.'

'No. I'm taking her down to Grandmother's tomorrow, in fact.'

'I am worried, Laurence.'

She looked worried. Her face had no confidence. There was a ladder in her stocking. She had said she wanted to see him urgently, and within the first five minutes she was coming to the point. There were other signs that she was very worried.

'I asked you to come, Laurence, because I'm so worried.'

He sat on the arm of her chair, he put his arm round her shoulder, and said,

'Is it to do with Caroline and me?'

'No,' she said.

Laurence got up and poured himself a drink. His mother had not offered him a drink. She was worried.

'Georgina Hogg came to see me yesterday.'

'Oh! What did she want?'

'I don't know. She told me an extraordinary story. I'm so worried.'

'About Caroline? I told you Caroline had left St Philumena's on Georgina Hogg's account. Can you blame her?'

'No, of course not.'

'You shouldn't have sent Caroline to that place. You know what Georgina's like.'

'Well, Father Jerome agreed –'

'But he doesn't know Georgina Hogg. You should never have given her that job. What took you to do that? She's such a frightful advertisement for the Church.'

'I just thought,' said Helena. 'One tries to be charitable. I thought. She said a miracle seemed to have brought her back to me. I thought, "Perhaps she has changed." One never knows, in our Faith. Anything can happen to anyone.'

'Well, Georgina hasn't changed apparently. Still the

same psychological thug as she always was. I think honestly she's to blame for Caroline's relapse. She must have touched a raw nerve.'

Helena said, 'Pour me a drink, Laurence.'

'What will you have?'

'Same as you.'

Laurence gave her a drink as strong as his own, which she didn't object to on this occasion.

'What's on your mind, darling? What does Georgina want now?'

'I don't know. She came to tell me something.'

'Felt it was her duty, as usual? What did she say about Caroline?'

'That's right, that's what she said, about it being her duty. She didn't say much about Caroline but she told me an extraordinary story about my mother going in for some terribly illegal business. She suggested that Mother was a receiver of stolen property.'

'My dear, what made her say that?'

Helena was apologetic. She didn't quite know how to tell Laurence what her protected servant had done.

'I don't quite know how to tell you, Laurence. I thought Georgina had changed. And of course she's got a justification, an excuse. Caroline didn't leave her address. She says a letter came for Caroline the day after she left. Georgina took upon herself to open it, just to see the address of the writer, she said, meaning to return it. Then she found the letter came from you. She read it, as she felt that was her duty to me. You see, Laurence, she has an excuse for everything.'

'But that's illegal. No one has any right to open a letter addressed to someone else. Only the Post Office can do that, when the person it's addressed to can't be traced. And even then, officially they only look at the signature and the address on the letter. No one *at all* has a right to read the substance of a letter addressed to someone else,' Laurence said. He was fairly raging.

'I told her that, Laurence. I'm worried, dear.'

'What did she mean, she felt it was her duty to you to read my letter to Caroline?'

'I don't know. Perhaps she thought there was something between you of which I wasn't aware. I put her right on that score.'

'Did you tell her it's a serious crime to do what she's done?' Laurence was on his third whisky.

'Hush, dear,' said his mother, forgetting his size, 'I don't know if we're in a position to talk about crime to Georgina Hogg. You must tell me all you know about Grandmother. You should have told me right away.'

'Did the Hogg show you my letter, or did she only tell you what I wrote?'

'She offered to let me read it. I refused.'

'Good,' said Laurence. 'That keeps our own standards up.'

His mother smiled a little and looked at him. But she returned to her anxiety. 'Georgina was very high-minded about what you wrote about *her*, whatever it was.'

'She didn't offer to return my letter to me, I suppose? It's my property.'

'No, she refused,' said Helena.

'And what's her excuse for *that*?'

'Feels it's her duty. She says that these things are too often hushed up.'

'Blackmail?' Laurence said.

'She didn't ask for anything,' said Helena. Then, as if these exchanges were so many tedious preliminaries, she said, as one getting down to business, 'Laurence, that was true wasn't it – what you wrote to Caroline about Grandmother?'

'Yes. But I don't think Grandmother's a criminal. I didn't say that. Possibly she's being used by a gang of criminals.' He did not sound very convinced of this.

Helena said, 'I've been blind. I've been simply inattentive these past four years since my father's death. I should have made it my business to look after my mother. I should have forced her to accept –'

73

'Where's Georgina now? Has she gone back?'

'No. She has given notice. I don't know where she's staying. I was too stunned to ask.'

'What is she going to do about the letter?'

'She said she would keep it, that's all.'

'What is she going to do about Grandmother?'

'She wouldn't say. Oh Laurence, I'm so worried about your grandmother. Tell me all about it. Tell me everything.'

'I don't know everything.'

'This about diamonds in the bread. I can't believe it, and yet Georgina was so serious. I like to know where I am. Tell me what you discovered.'

'All right,' Laurence said. He knew that his mother had a peculiar faith that no evil could touch her. It made her adaptable to new ideas. Laurence had seen her coming round to one after another acceptance where his own vagaries were concerned. Especially now, when she sat worried in her shabby drawing-room, wearing her well-worn blue with the quite expensive pearls, a ladder in her stocking, Laurence thought, 'She could get through a jungle without so much as a scratch.'

When he had finished talking she said, 'When will you leave for Ladylees?'

'Tomorrow, as early as possible. By train; my car's going in for repair. I'll hire one at Hayward's Heath for the few days.'

'Don't take Caroline.'

'Why not?'

'She isn't strong enough, surely, to be mixed up in this?'

'I should say it would do her good.'

'She will be in your way, surely, if you intend making inquiries.'

'Not Caroline. She's too cute.'

'Tell Caroline to keep in touch with me, then. Ask her to phone every day and let me know what's happening. I can depend on Caroline.'

'Whisky makes you snooty,' he said. 'You can depend on me too.'

'Wheedle the truth out of your grandmother,' she pleaded.

As he started to leave, she said shyly in case there should be any offence, 'Try to find out how much it will cost us to get her out of the hands of these crooks.'

Laurence said, 'We don't know who's in whose hands, really. Better not mention it to Father just yet; it may turn out to be something quite innocent, a game of Grandmother's –'

'I won't trouble your father just yet,' she assured him abruptly. 'He does so admire my mother.' Then she added, 'To think that our old trusted servant should do a thing like this.'

He thought that a bit of hypocrisy – that 'old trusted servant' phrase.

'You think I'm a hypocrite, don't you?' his mother said.

'Of course not,' he replied, 'why should I?'

'Everything O.K.?'

Caroline woke at the sound of Laurence's voice. She was very sleepy still; this protracted waking up was also a sign that she was getting better. Muzzily, she was not sure if Laurence had said 'Everything O.K.?' or if this was something as yet unspoken, which it was her place to ask. So she said, all muzzed, sitting up, 'Everything O.K.?'

Laurence laughed.

She rose sleepily and went into the bathroom to wash and change, leaving the door open to talk through.

'Any incidents?' said Laurence.

She was awake now. 'Yes,' she told him. 'Lord Tom Noddy on the air.'

'Who?'

'Madame Butterfly.'

'And did you remember the tape-machine?'

'Um. I pressed the button. But I don't know if it's recorded anything.'

She sounded diffident. Laurence said:

'Shall I try?' He was afraid the experiment might upset her, might turn the luck of Caroline's health.

'Yes, do.'

He arranged the recording device, and pressed a lever. It gave a tiny whirr, then came the boom of Laurence's voice. 'Caroline darling ...' followed by the funny, unprintable suggestion.

Caroline came out of the bathroom to listen, towel in hand. They were both eager for the next bit. It was a woman's voice. Laurence looked up sharply as it spoke: 'That's a damned lie. You're getting scared, I think. Why are you suddenly taking cover under that protestation?'

That was all. 'Good Christ!' said Laurence.

Caroline explained, rather embarrassed. 'That was my voice, answering back. It seems, my dear, that these visiting voices don't record. I didn't really think they would take.'

'What did they say to you? Why did you reply like that? What made you say "It's a lie"?'

She read him the shorthand notes she had taken.

'So you see,' she said with a hurt laugh, 'the characters are all fictitious.'

Laurence fiddled absently with the machine. When she stopped talking, he told her to hurry and get dressed. He kissed her as if she were a child.

As she made up her face she told him excitably, 'I have the answer. I know how to handle that voice.'

She expected him to ask, 'Tell me how.' But he didn't; he looked at her, still reckoning her in his regard as if she were a lovable child.

Then he said, 'Mother's worried. I'm afraid there's going to be a big shemozzle about Grandmother.'

It seemed to Laurence, then, that it was unsatisfactory for Caroline to be a child. He felt the need of her coordinating mind to piece together the mysterious facts of his grandmother's life. He felt helpless.

'You'll help me with my grandmother, won't you?' he said.

'Why?' she said gaily. 'What are you going to do to your grandmother?' She looked mock-sinister. She was getting better. Laurence looked from her face to the shorthand notebook on the table, from the evidence of her normality to the evidence of her delusion. Perhaps, he thought, a person could go through life with one little crank and remain perfectly normal in every other respect. Perhaps it was only in regard to the imaginary aural impressions that Caroline was a child.

He said, 'Mrs Hogg read the letter I sent to you at St Philumena's.'

'You mean, she opened my letter and read it?'

'Yes, it's appalling. In fact, it's criminal.'

Caroline smiled a little at this. Laurence remembered the same sort of smile fleeting on his mother's face that afternoon in spite of her worry. He realized what it was the two women had smiled the same smile about.

'I admit that I've read other people's letters myself. I quite see that. But this is a difference case. It's frightful, actually.'

Having established, with her smile, the fact that she considered him not altogether adult, Caroline said, 'On the level, is it serious?' And she began to question him as an equal.

They switched off the fires and light, still talking, and left the flat.

At about half past eleven, since they had decided to make a night of it, they went to dance at a place called the Pylon in Dover Street. There was hardly any light, and Caroline thought, Thank God for that.

For, after dinner at a restaurant in Knightsbridge, they had been to Soho. First, to a pub where some B.B.C. people were unexpectedly forgathered who called Laurence 'Larry'; and this was a washout so far as Laurence was concerned. His mind was on his grandmother, and the spoiling of his disinterestedness, his peace, by Mrs Hogg. He was on leave, moreover, and did not reckon to meet with his colleagues in those weeks. Next they had gone to a literary pub, where it rapidly became clear that the Baron had spread the story of Caroline and her hysterical night at his flat.

At the first pub, after they had left, a friend of Laurence had said, 'That's Larry's form of perversion – beautiful neurotic women. They have to be neurotic.'

It was understood that every close association between two people was a perversion. Caroline sensed the idea they had left behind them when they left this pub. Laurence, of course, knew it, but he didn't mind; he accepted that, for instance, 'perversion' was his friends' code-word for any-one's personal taste in love. While Caroline and Laurence were on their way to the second pub, this friend of Laurence's was saying, 'All Larry's girls have been neurotics.' This was true, as it happened.

Later, in the taxi, Caroline said to Laurence, 'Am I noticeably neurotic, do you think?'

Her eyes were huge and deep, unsettled, but she had the power of judgement in other features of her face.

He said, 'Yes, in a satisfactory way.' And he said presently, 'All my girls have been neurotics.'

Caroline knew this but was glad to hear it again from Laurence; his words made articulate her feeling of what was being said in the pub they had left. She knew most of Laurence's previous neurotic girls; she herself was the enduring one.

Presently again, and Laurence said,

'There are more interesting particulars about neurotic women. You never know what you mayn't find on their persons and in their general carry-on.'

In the second pub, where a fair fat poet said to Caro-line, 'Tell me *all* about your visions, my dear'; and another poet, a woman with a cape and a huge mouth, said, 'Is there much Satanism going on within the Catholic Church these days?'; and another sort of writer, a man of over fifty, asked Caroline who was her psycho-analyst, and told her who was his – at this pub Caroline collected, one way and another, that the Baron had been mentioning this and that about her, to the ageless boys and girls who dropped in on him at his bookshop in Charing Cross Road.

The fat poet went steadily on about Caroline's 'visions'; he said they would be good for her publicity. Caroline and Laurence had been on short drinks, and both were rather lit up.

'Wonderful publicity,' they both agreed.

And the over-fifty, in his brown coat of fur-fabric, persisted,

'I could tell you of a psychiatrist who –'

'We know one,' Laurence said, 'who analyses crazy pavements.'

Caroline told the girl in the cape, did she know that Eleanor Hogarth had deserted the Baron?

'No!'

'Yes. He put me up for the night at his flat last week. All her things were gone. Not even a photograph. He only mentioned her once. He said she was away on tour, which was true; he said nothing about the break. Then Laurence found out definitely – he finds out everything, of course.'

'Gone off with someone else?'

'Don't know, really. But she's left him, not he her; I know that.'

'Poor Willi.'

'Oh, one can't blame her,' said Caroline, satisfied that the story would now spread.

The girl in the cape said, 'Have you tried to convert the Baron?'

'Me? No.'

'R.C.s usually try to convert everyone, however hopeless. I thought that was a sort of obligation.'

For good measure, Caroline quoted of the Baron what she heard said of someone else: 'He exhausted his capacity for conversion when he became an Englishman.'

Indeed, the Baron was rather scrupulous about his English observances and confident that he had the English idea, so that his contempt for the English, their intellect, their manners, arose from a vexation that they did not conform better to the idea. To this effect, Caroline exchanged her views on the Baron with the girl in the cape.

'But you know,' said the girl, 'there's another side to Willi Stock. He's an orgiast on the quiet.'

'A what?'

'Goes in for the Black Mass. He's a Satanist. Probably that's why Eleanor left him. She's so awfully bourgeois.'

Caroline suddenly felt oppressed by the pub and the people. That word 'bourgeois' had a dispiriting effect on her evening – it was part of the dreary imprecise language of this half-world she had left behind her more than two years since.

Laurence was talking to the blond fat poet who was inviting him to a party at someone else's house next week, describing the sort of people who would be present; and as Caroline got up, Laurence caught her eye just as this man was saying, 'You can't afford to miss it.'

Laurence piloted her out to the taxi, for she had been wobbly even when they arrived. But the momentary revulsion had sobered her.

They went to a coffee house, then on to the West End, to the Pylon, where, Caroline thought, thank God the lights are dim and the people not too distinguishable. The West End was another half-world of Caroline's past.

Eleanor Hogarth had a close look at the couple moving in the sleepy gloom before her. They had a square foot of floor-space, which they utilized with sweet skill, within its scope manoeuvring together like creatures out of natural history. This fascinated Eleanor; she was for a few moments incredulous at the sight of Caroline and Laurence in these surroundings, since she had never seen them before in a night-club, nor dancing.

Eleanor waved from her table; it was too far away from

them to call, decently. Eventually Caroline saw. 'Oh, see, there's Eleanor.'

And there she was, with her business partner, white-haired young-faced Ernest Manders. This was Laurence's uncle, his father's youngest brother who had gone into ballet instead of Manders' Figs in Syrup.

When Laurence was quite little he had informed his mother,

'Uncle Ernest is a queer.'

'So he is, pet,' she answered happily, and repeated the child's words to several people before she learned from her husband the difference between being a queer and just being queer. After this, it became a family duty to pray for Uncle Ernest; it was understood that no occasion for prayers should pass without a mention of this uncle. And with some success apparently, because in his fortieth year, when his relations with men were becoming increasingly violent, he gave them up for comfort's sake; not that he ever took to women as a substitute. Laurence had re-marked to Caroline one day,

'I've gradually had to overcome an early disrespect for my Uncle Ernest.'

'Because he was a homosexual?'

'No. Because we were always praying specially for him.'

He was a religious man and likeable. Caroline got on well with him. She said he was her sort of Catholic, critical but conforming. Ernest always agreed with Caroline that the True Church was awful, though unfortunately, one couldn't deny, true.

She could not much bear Eleanor these days, though it was through Eleanor that she had first met Laurence. At one time these women were friends, exceedingly of a kind; that was at Cambridge, when, in their boxy rooms, they had leaned on the ignoble wooden fittings which were stained with rings from cocoa-mugs, and talked of this and that; mostly about the insolence of their fellow students and the insolence of their elders, for both girls had potential talents unrecognized. They were united in discontentment with the place as a place; its public-tiled wash-rooms, its bed-sitting-rooms, and other apartments so insolently designed. Eleanor left after a couple of terms to go into ballet. She might easily have gone to an art school, for she also had the art-school gift. It was Eleanor who had removed from one of the ground-floor corridors, and from its place on a wall, the portrait of a former Principal, keeping it for a whole night, in the course of which, by means of innumerable small touchings, she had made a subtle and important alteration in the portrait, which remains undetected to this day.

The thing about Eleanor, Caroline held, was that her real talent was for mimicry, and so she could have taken up any trade with ease, because all she had to do was to mimic the best that had already been done in any particular line, and that gave the impression of the expert.

Caroline was abroad during Eleanor's marriage; she did not know much about it, only that she had left her husband after the war, and under her married name had started a dancing school with a male partner. Ernest Manders. A few months later, Caroline and Laurence had set up together, by which time Eleanor's relationship with the Baron was becoming established. What irritated Caroline now about her old friend was the fact that she had seemed not to change essentially in the years since their Cambridge days, and was apparently quite happy with herself as she was. Now Laurence was another like that. But Caroline could like in Laurence many characteristics which in others she could not tolerate. And she was aware of the irrationality and prejudice of all these feelings, without being able to stop feeling them.

But she said, so that her contempt for Eleanor should be concealed,

'Look at the band-leader. Who does he look like?' She mentioned a Cambridge don, with his rimless glasses and the sideways mouth. Eleanor laughed and laughed. She had been drinking more than Caroline that evening. 'So he does.' Then she told Caroline a story from which it emerged that this don was dead.

'I didn't know that,' said Caroline, being shocked then that Eleanor had laughed at her joke. When she saw Caroline involuntarily putting her face serious, Eleanor affirmed, 'But the band boy is the image of the man, just the same.'

Then Eleanor started picking out other members of the band, likening them to men they had agreed in despising during their friendship days. And she got Caroline to laugh, putting their meeting on a basis of workable humour, considering they were supposed to be enjoying themselves: and this was only possible by reference to the one kindly association between the two women, their college friendship. Caroline got over her annoyance at being caught out putting on a grave religious face when Eleanor had laughed at a dead man. And while she entered into Eleanor's amusement, she felt almost dumb about her suspicion that Eleanor was humouring her on account of her neurosis. She was right; this was exactly Eleanor's idea as she sat with her dark-brown head leaning over towards Caroline's much darker brown.

Two bottles of gin had appeared out of the gloom. Laurence, on his third drink from the first bottle, said,

'I've never felt more sober in my life. Some occasions, it just won't "take", you simply can't get drunk.'

Eleanor looked sorry for him, as if she knew he had worry on his mind from Caroline. This annoyed Caroline, because she knew he was worrying about his grandmother most of all.

While she danced with Ernest, who was weird to dance with, flexible, almost not there at all, so that she felt like a missile directed from a far distance, she saw Laurence examining Eleanor's cigarette case in his nosey way, and thought, 'He keeps trying to detect whatever it is he's looking for in life.' She admired his ability to start somewhere repeatedly; his courage; even if it was only in a cigarette case.

Soon, Laurence and Eleanor were dancing, then she saw that they sat down, and that Eleanor was talking in a confiding way; Eleanor was making small circular movements with her glass, stopping only to sigh reflectively into it before she drank, as often happens towards the end of a drinking night, when a woman confides in a man about another man.

Round the walls of the Pylon, so far as the walls could be discerned, were large gilt picture frames. Inside each, where the picture should be, was a square of black velvet, this being the Pylon's sort of effectiveness. As she smoothed her slight feet with Ernest, so limp, over their portion of dancing-floor, Caroline caught her view of Eleanor's head, described against one of the black squares of velvet in the background, just like a framed portrait, indistinct, in need of some touching-up.

Chapter 5

'I SAID, "Willi, this can't go on, it simply can not go on." '
Eleanor was getting maudlin. She was not a neurotic particularly, but that was not why Laurence didn't much care
for her. It was only that he rather liked the Baron, and
Eleanor, though her infidelities were her own affair, had
never kept very quiet about them, except to the Baron
himself who never suspected them.

Laurence, gazing intently at her small gold cigarette
case as if it were the book of life itself, nodded his acknow-
ledgement of her confidences.

'If he had been unfaithful,' she went on, 'I could have
understood, I could have forgiven. But this obscenity –
and apparently it's been going on for years – I never suspected. Of course I always knew he was interested in diabolism and that sort of thing, but I thought it was only
theory. He had all the books, and I thought like a collector
you know. But apparently it's been going on for years, the
Black Masses, and they do frightful things, ask Caroline,
she'll know all about the Black Mass. I feel it's a sort of
personal insult to me personally, as if I'd found him out
dabbling with a whore. And I said, "Willi, you've got to
choose, it's either me or these foul practices – you can't
have both." Because I tell you, Laurence, it was an insult
to my intelligence apart from everything else. He said he
was amused by my attitude. Amused. I'm not melodra-
matic, and further*more*, I'm not religious, but I do know
that the Black Mass has a profoundly evil influence truly,
Laurence. In fact, I wouldn't be surprised if he hasn't
done something to Caroline.'

'How d'you mean, dear?'

'Well, I don't know if it's true, but I heard that she
spent a night with Willi recently –'

'Yes, he was sweet to her really. She was ill at the time.

But I think that was the climax, somehow. I think she's getting better now.'

'But I heard that she started hearing things after that night. I heard that and you can't help hearing things when people tell you, however unlikely.'

Laurence did not quite get the hang of this sentence, and while he was working it out Eleanor persisted,

'Hasn't Caroline been hearing things?'

'About you, dear?'

'No, voices. Spirits. Hearing –'

'Come and dance,' said Laurence.

This was their second attempt. She was even less steady than before, and it took him all his time to keep her upright. He said, 'Too many people, what d'you think?'

'Yes,' she said, 'let's sit down and drink.'

Ernest and Caroline were already returned. Eleanor said immediately, 'Caroline, what do you think of the Black Mass?'

Caroline's mood had become gay and physical; she was still jiggering about with her hands in time to the music. 'No idea,' she answered, 'but ask the Baron. He's the expert, so I'm told.' Then she remembered that Eleanor had left the Baron, so she said, 'Laurence, stop peering at Eleanor's cigarette case, like an old Jew looking for the carat mark.'

Laurence said, 'I'm trying to read the motto.'

On the front of the case was a tiny raised crest. Caroline poked her head in beside Laurence's with exaggerated curiosity. 'A wolf's head,' said Laurence. 'What's the motto? I can't read it.'

'*Fidelis et* – I can't remember, for the moment,' Eleanor said. 'I did know. It's the Hogarth crest. Only a Victorian rake-up, I imagine. My ex-husband gave me that case for a wedding present. He had a passion for putting his family crest on everything. Spoons, hairbrushes, you never saw the like. Caroline, seriously, don't you think the evil influence that's over us all is due to these Black Masses? I've found out about Willi. I suppose you've known all the time, but I didn't dream. And it takes place at Notting Hill Gate, as you probably know.'

Laurence had given her a weak drink, but now, sipping it, she noticed this, and said to Ernest reproachfully, 'I'm drinking lemonade, virtually. Don't be so mean with that gin, Ernest.'

Caroline was fascinated by Eleanor's performance. Indeed, it was only an act; the fascination of Eleanor was her entire submersion in whatever role she had to play. There did not seem to be any question of Eleanor's choosing her part, it was forced on her, she was enslaved by it. Just now, she appeared to be under the control of liquor; but she was also and more completely under the control of her stagey act: that of a scatty female who'd been drinking: wholeheartedly, her personality was involved, so that it was impossible to distinguish between Eleanor and the personality which possessed her during those hours; as well try to distinguish between the sea and the water in it.

Caroline was fascinated and appalled. In former days, Eleanor's mimicry was recognizable. She would change her personality like dresses according to occasion, and it had been fun to watch, and an acknowledged joke of Eleanor's. But she had lost her small portion of detachment; now, to watch her was like watching doom. As a child Caroline, pulling a face, had been warned, 'If you keep doing that it will stick one day.' She felt, looking at Eleanor, that this was actually happening to the woman. Her assumed personalities were beginning to cling; soon one of them would stick, grotesque and ineradicable.

'She's got the Black Mass on the brain,' Ernest was sighing.

'So would you if you'd been living with a diabolist,' said Eleanor, contorting her face according to her role of the moment. And she drawled, placing a hand on Caroline's hand, looking intensely into her eyes,

'Caroline, my poor Caroline. You're haunted by spirits, aren't you? And you know who's behind it, don't you?'

The performance was becoming more and more corny. Caroline tried to revert to their earlier farce about the band and their Cambridge friends.

'But she's haunted,' said Eleanor, still gazing at Caroline.

Caroline had never felt less haunted. She was almost shocked to find how she seemed to derive composure from the evidence of her friend's dissolution.

'I've never felt less haunted,' Caroline said.

'*I'm* haunted,' said Ernest, 'by the fact that we're nearly bankrupt, and Eleanor has abandoned our only form of security.'

'Willi can't withdraw financially. But he'll ruin us all another way. I know it. I feel it. He's working a tremendous power against us,' Eleanor drivelled.

'What was your husband's name?' Laurence asked her.

'You *are* haunted, my dear girl,' Eleanor insisted, still gazing upon Caroline's face.

'Hogarth.' It was Ernest who supplied the name, smiling like a conjurer who has produced the rabbit.

'Mervyn,' said Eleanor belatedly.

'I believe I've met him. Does he live at Ladle Sands in Sussex by any chance?'

'Yes,' said Eleanor. 'Don't remind me *please*. He ought to be in prison. I've had a tragic life, Laurence. Ernest, haven't I had a tragic life?'

'Desperately,' said Ernest.

'And the tragedy of that poor cripple boy,' said Eleanor. 'Caroline, I've never told you about my marriage. What a mess. He had a son by a former marriage, quite helpless. What could I do? These tragedies occur everywhere through influences of evil spirits, that I do believe. You've given me sheer *lemonade*, Ernest, don't be mean with the gin.'

'You're getting tight,' said Ernest.

'Can you blame me? Caroline, do you realize the sheer potency of the Black Mass? It's going on all the time.'

'I shouldn't worry,' said Caroline. 'It's only an infantile orgy. It can't do much harm.'

'Have you ever been to a Black Mass?'

'No. It takes me all my time to keep up with the white Mass on Sundays.'

'What's the white Mass? Ernest, tell me what's the white Mass?'

'She means the Mass, dear. The ordinary Catholic Mass,' Ernest said.

'Oh, but this is different. The Black Mass has tremendous power. It can actually make objects move. Nobody touches them. They move. I've read heaps about it. There are naked girls, and they say everything backward. And obscenity. Ernest, you don't take me seriously, but you just *go* to a Black Mass, and see. I challenge you. *I* wouldn't dare go. I'd die.'

Caroline and Laurence spoke simultaneously, 'Catholics can't go to Black Masses.'

'Not allowed,' Ernest explained.

'They treat you like kids,' said Eleanor, 'don't they, Laurence?' she said, for she knew he had lapsed from religion.

'That's right,' he said agreeably.

'Why is the Black Mass forbidden, if there isn't some tremendous evil in it?' she persisted, her hand on Caroline's.

'I don't say there isn't great evil in it,' Caroline replied, 'I only say it's a lot of tomfoolery.'

'I wouldn't dismiss it so lightly as that,' Ernest argued.

'It depends on how you regard evil,' Caroline said. 'I mean, as compared with the power of goodness. The effectuality of the Black Mass, for instance, must be trivial so long as we have the real Mass.'

'I wouldn't dismiss the power of evil lightly,' Ernest insisted. 'It does exist, obviously.'

'I thought,' said Eleanor, 'that Catholics all believed the same thing. But I can see you don't.'

'Caroline is being mystical,' Ernest said.

'Caroline is a mystic,' said Eleanor. 'I've always said so. She's a mystic, isn't she, Laurence?'

'Every time,' said Laurence, very pleasantly.

'And the trouble with these mystics, they theorise on the basis of other people's sufferings, and in the end they belittle suffering. Caroline, if you'd suffered as much as I've suffered, you wouldn't be talking like something out of this world.'

'I won't compete with you on the question of suffering,' Caroline spoke acidly, for, after all, she rather fancied herself as a sufferer.

'Poor girl, you are haunted by the evil ones,' Eleanor said, which was maddening just at that moment.

'I shouldn't have much to do with Willi,' Eleanor continued. 'Take my advice and keep clear.'

'Poor Willi!' Caroline said with a happy laugh, though meaning malice.

'The Baron is charming, bless him,' said Laurence, in an absent way, for he was conferring with Ernest over paying their bill.

'Willi makes his money out of the Black Mass,' Eleanor stated. 'That's where he gets it from, I'm sure.'

'Oh, surely it can't be a business matter?' Laurence put in again.

'They do quite a trade in consecrated wafers,' said Eleanor.

'In *what*?' Caroline said, seriously disturbed for the first time since the subject was mentioned.

Laurence said, 'I doubt if they make a point of the wafers being consecrated.'

'I believe they do,' Ernest said. 'I'm afraid that seems to be the whole point of the Black Mass.'

'It's a very rare thing these days,' Caroline said. 'Satanism fizzled out in the twenties.'

'Oh, did it?' Eleanor said, getting ready to argue the point.

Laurence interrupted with, 'Why did you say your ex-husband should be in prison?'

'Mind y'r own business, lovey.' Eleanor screwed up her face into an inebriate smile.

'Is there a relation of his, do you know, called Georgina Hogg?'

'I can see,' said Caroline, 'we've reached the stage where each one discourses upon his private obsession, regardless –'

'I just wondered,' Laurence explained, 'because that crest on Eleanor's cigarette case is the same as the one on some of Georgina's possessions.'

Eleanor did not reply. She had a look of drunken incoherence which may have covered any emotion.

'Possibly derived from the same name, originally,' Caroline suggested: ' "Hogg" and "Hogarth".'

When they went to get their coats Caroline had to take Eleanor's arm to keep her steady, although she felt a slight electricity singing in her own limbs. In the cloakroom Eleanor revived a little, and putting on her lipstick shifted over her attitude to the woman-to-woman basis.

'Men are clods.

'And keep away, Caroline, do, from the Baron.

'And Laurence said something about a woman called Hogg? I couldn't quite catch – I'm so sleepy, so tight.' In evidence, she yawned with her mouth all over her face.

Caroline replied with exaggerated precision, annoyed at having to repeat what Eleanor already knew.

'Yes. She was a nursemaid or governess with the Manders years ago. Laurence thought there might be some connection between her and your husband because the crest on your cigarette case is the same as the crest on Mrs Hogg's possessions, apparently.'

'A nursemaid with a family crest?'

'Apparently. It's quite possible,' said Caroline.

'There may be some original connection between the names "Hogg" and "Hogarth",' Eleanor said, as if she had not heard Caroline's remark to this effect, and had just thought of it herself.

91

'Quite,' said Caroline, and noticed that this abrupt finality did not have a satisfying effect on Eleanor.

As they waited for their coats Eleanor asked,

'Where are you living now?'

'In Queen's Gate, quite near our old flat.'

'And Laurence?'

'Laurence is still in the old flat.'

'Officially, that is?' said Eleanor.

'What d'you mean?'

'Well, dear Carrie, I heard that Laurence couldn't tear himself away from you, and was stopping over at your new place.'

'Oh, that's only a temporary arrangement. I haven't been well.'

'A temporary arrangement! You Roman Catholics can get away with anything. You just nip into the confessional in between temporary arrangements, so to speak.'

'We sleep in separate rooms, as it happens.' Then Caroline was furious with herself for making this defence where none was due. Laurence wouldn't like it, either. 'I rate friendship infinitely higher than erotic love,' she added, trying to improve matters, but making them worse.

They found Laurence and Ernest outside with a taxi.

'Let's walk a little way and get some air,' Caroline said to Laurence.

'Oh, then we'll walk with you. That would be nice,' said Eleanor.

But Ernest, with his tact, got her into the cab. Before they said good night, Eleanor, slurred and mouthy, declared, 'Now, Laurence, take care of Caroline. She's just been telling me that you both sleep in separate rooms. It's a good story if you stick to it. And it must be a frightful strain either way. No wonder Caroline's haunted.'

They left London next day by car, though Laurence's M.G. was overdue for repair, instead of going by train. This was owing to their getting up late and frittering the day in talk, first about poor Eleanor, as they agreed she was, then about themselves.

Caroline had not slept much that night. To start with it was after four o'clock by the time she parted from Laurence who was sleeping on a camp bed in the kitchen. She lay awake for about half an hour and then she was visited by the voices, preceded by the typewriter. This was the first time it had happened while Laurence was in the flat.

As soon as she heard the familiar tapping she called softly to Laurence; he was quite near, only a few yards away through the open door.

'Are you awake?'

He was instantly awake. 'Yes?'

'Don't come. Only listen. Here's that noise again. Keep quiet.'

It had already started its chanting. She switched on the light and grabbed her notebook and pencil. She missed the first bit, but she got:

'. . . next day by car, though Laurence's M.G. was due for repair, instead of going by train. This was owing to their getting up late and frittering the day in talk, first about poor Eleanor, as they agreed she was, then about themselves. Click. Click.

'Did you hear that?' Caroline then called out to Laurence.

'No, my dear, I didn't hear a thing.'

He had got out of bed and now came in, looking anxious. 'Are you all right?'

She was sitting up, gazing at her shorthand notes.

'I can't make this out,' she said. 'I can't make it out at all.'

She read it to him.

'You're thinking ahead. Don't worry about tomorrow. We can sleep late and catch an afternoon train.'

'I didn't imagine these words. They were told me,' she stated, but unprotesting factually.

'Shall I come in beside you?'

'Make some tea first.'

He did this, while Caroline continued gazing at the notebook.

When he brought their tea, he said, 'I'll come in beside you.'

It was a three-quarter divan and so there was just room. Caroline considered the situation as she drank her tea, then she said,

'I'll be all right by myself, really I will.'

'It's cold in the kitchen,' said Laurence.

He began to snuggle down.

'I'll put a pillow down the middle,' Caroline said.

'Wouldn't a bread-knife and a prayer book do instead?'

'Clear off,' said Caroline.

'All I want is a beautiful night's sleep.'

'Same here,' she said.

Eventually they brought in the camp bed from the kitchen and settled down alongside. He reflected how strangely near impracticable sexual relations would be between them, now that Caroline thought them sinful. She was thinking the same thing.

It was past eleven when they woke next morning.

It was while they cooked their omelettes for lunch that she told Laurence, as if it were an undeniable fact, of her theory about the author making a book out of their lives.

Laurence knew that people with obsessions could usually find evidence to fit their craziest convictions. From the time he had learned about the voices, he had been debating within himself what this might mean to his relationship with Caroline. He had hoped that the failure of the tape-machine to record the sounds would prove her delusion to her. And when this failed to impress her he wondered whether it would be possible for him to humour her fantasy indefinitely, so that she could be the same Caroline except for this one difference in their notions of reality; or whether reality would force them apart, and the time arrive when he needs must break with, 'Caroline, you are wrong, mistaken, mad. There are no voices; there is no typewriter; it is all a delusion. You must get mental treatment.'

It was on his tongue to tell her so when, standing in her dressing-gown cooking the eggs and bacon, she told him, 'I've discovered the truth of the matter'; the truth of the matter being, it transpired, this fabulous idea of themselves and their friends being used as characters in a novel.

'How do you know it's a novel?'

' "The characters in this novel are all fictitious," ' she quoted with a truly mad sort of laugh.

'In fact,' she continued, 'I've begun to study the experience objectively. That's a sign, isn't it, that I'm well again?'

He thought not. He went so far to suggest, 'Your work on the novel form – isn't it possible that your mind –'

'It's convenient that I know something of the novel form,' Caroline said.

'Yes,' he said.

He argued a little, questioned her. Was the author disembodied? – She didn't know. If so, how could he use a typewriter? How could she overhear him? How could one author chant in chorus? – That she didn't know, that she didn't know. Was the author human or a spirit, and if so –

'How can I answer these questions? I've only begun to ask them myself. The author obviously exists in a different dimension from ours. That will make the investigation difficult.'

He realized, then, that he was arguing madness upon madness, was up against a private revelation. He almost wished he were still a believer, so that he could the more forcefully use some Catholic polemic against her privacy.

'From the Catholic point of view, I should have thought there were spiritual dangers in holding this conviction.'

'There are spiritual dangers in everything. From the Catholic point of view the chief danger about a conviction is the temptation to deny it.'

'But you ought to subject it to reason.'

'I'm doing so,' Caroline said. 'I have started investigations,' and she was becoming delighted with this talk.

He said then, 'Don't you think the idea of an invisible person tuning in to your life might possibly upset your faith?'

'Of course,' she said. 'That's why he ought to be subjected to reason!'

'Well,' he said wearily, 'I've never heard of a Catholic being allowed to traffic with the unknown like this.'

'The author is doing all the trafficking,' she explained. 'But I'm going to make it difficult for him, you'll see.'

'The whole thing is far too gnostic,' he said.

That did amuse her. 'That does amuse me,' she said; 'you expressing yourself so orthodox.'

'It makes damn all difference to me if you're a heretic, darling, because you're sweet. But sooner or later you'll come bump against authority. Did you tell Father Jerome about this idea?'

'I mentioned the possibility. I had only just realized it.'

'Didn't he object?'

'No, why should he? It isn't a sin to be a little cracked in the head.' She added, 'I know that I am slightly insane.'

'No,' he said gently, 'you are quite sane, Caroline.'

'From your point of view,' she insisted, 'I am out of my senses. It would be a human indignity to deny it.'

He thought, How cunning of her to get round it that way, and he remembered that with madness comes cunning.

'You have a mild nervous disorder,' he said.

'I have what you ought to call a delusion. In any normal opinion that's a fact.'

'Caroline, don't distress yourself, dear.'

'The normal opinion is bound to distress me because it's a fact like the fact of the author and the facts of the Faith. They are all painful to me in different ways.'

'What can I do?' he said, as he had said many times in the past days. 'What can I do to help you?'

'Will you be able to make an occasional concession to the logic of my madness?' she asked him. 'Because that will be necessary between us. Otherwise, we shall be really separated.' She was terrified of being entirely separated from Laurence.

'Haven't I always tried to enter your world?'

'Yes, but this is a very remote world I'm in now.'

'Not really,' he said. 'You're as good as normal in every other way.'

He wondered if she was hurt by this. He wondered he had not courage enough to make her see a mental doctor.

She said, 'We shall have to keep this secret. I don't want the reputation of being crackers more than necessary. The Baron has broadcast enough already.'

It was a pact. But less than a couple of hours later he saw how irksome it could be.

They had already frittered the best part of the day, and it was past four when Laurence, after telephoning the station about the trains, said,

'We'd better go by car. It's O.K. for the one trip, and I can get it seen to at Hayward's Heath quite quickly. Then we can have the use of it, much more convenient.'

'Oh, you can hire a car at Hayward's Heath,' Caroline said quickly. 'I want to go by train. We must go by train.'

'Don't be awkward. Get dressed, and I'll get the car out. Trains are hateful if you have the alternative of a car.'

'Awkward is just what I'm going to be,' Caroline said. She started hunting for her notebook.

'I've just jerked up to the fact,' she said, 'that our day is doing what the voices said it would. Now, we chatted about Eleanor. Then about ourselves. All right. We've frittered the day. The narrative says we went by car; all right, we must go by train. You do see that, don't you, Laurence? It's a matter of asserting free will.'

He quite saw. He thought, 'Why the hell should we be enslaved by her secret fantasy?'

'I don't see,' he said, 'why we should be inconvenienced by it one way or another. Let's act naturally.'

But he saw that Caroline had it very much on the brain that her phantom should be outwitted in this one particular.

'Very well,' he said. He felt his honesty under threat of strangling. He desired their relationship to continue with the least possible change, but ever since her conversion it had been altering. Laurence could not feel that they were further apart than before, but he felt, now, that Caroline was on shifting ground, liable to be swept beyond his reach at any moment. He was not sure if he was agile enough to keep contact with her, nor that the effort would be worth it beyond a point at which Caroline might become unrecognizable.

These misgivings nearly choked him while he said to Caroline,

'All right, we'll go by train.'

But when, at this, she turned gay, he thought predominantly, 'She will help me with Grandmother in spite of her illness. The holiday will be good for Caroline. We still need each other.' Also he thought, 'I love the girl.' And his excitement at the thought of unravelling his grandmother's mysteries somehow made Caroline more lovable.

She was dressed and had packed for them both, to make up to Laurence for his concession. It was half past five. Laurence was telephoning a wire to his grandmother, to expect them about eight o'clock.

'She probably prepared lunch,' he said, as he put down the receiver.

'Laurence, that's too bad of us.'

'But she'll be so happy when we arrive, she won't say a word. Are you ready?'

Standing by her desk when he had finished phoning, Laurence had torn a few outdated pages off the calendar.

'That brings you up to date,' he said.

98

She remarked ruefully, 'I tear off the weeks automatically, when I'm sitting at the desk. It's a reproach when the calendar gets behind the times. Really, I must get down to my book soon.'

They were ready to leave. Laurence lifted the suitcases. But she was still staring at the calendar.

'What's today?' she asked. 'It isn't November the first, is it?'

'That's right. November already. Do make haste.'

'All Saints' Day,' she continued, 'you know what that means?'

Like most people who are brought up in the Catholic faith, Laurence was quick in recollecting such things. 'A Holiday of Obligation,' he said.

'And I haven't been to Mass!'

'Oh, it can't be helped. Don't worry. It isn't considered a mortal sin if you genuinely forgot.'

'But I'm obliged to attend a Mass if there's an opportunity, since I have remembered. There's probably a late Mass at the Oratory. Probably at six-thirty. I'll have to go to that. You do see that, don't you, Laurence?'

'Yes, I quite see that.' So he did; he found it easy to see the obligations of the Catholic religion; it was part of his environment. He found it much easier to cope with Caroline's new-found Catholicism than her new-found psychicism. He also found it easy to say,

'We can't let Grandmother down again. Wouldn't that be a valid excuse for missing Mass?'

And he quite expected her reply,

'You go ahead by car, and I'll come by a later train.'

And therefore, happy at regaining his liberty on the question of taking his car, he said with ease,

'It would be more fun if we both went by car after your Mass. We could make it by eight o'clock.'

She felt relieved on the whole. Her great desire to travel by train was dispersed by the obvious necessities of going to Mass, and of not messing Laurence around any further.

Presently he said, 'Sure you won't mind,' for he under-

99

stood the question was safely settled for her, and he did not wish to play the tyrant. So he had the luxury of asking her several times, 'Quite sure, dear, it's all right? You don't mind coming by car?'

'After all,' she told him, 'it isn't a moral defeat. The Mass is a proper obligation. But to acquiesce in the requirements of someone's novel would have been ignoble.'

He gave academic consideration to this statement and observed, 'The acquiescence is accidental, in which sense the nobility must oblige.'

She thought, 'The hell of it, he understands that much. Why isn't he a Catholic, then?' She smiled at him over her drink, for their immediate haste was over and Laurence had fished out the bottle which she had packed in his suitcase, very carefully in its proper corner.

Brompton Oratory oppressed her when it was full of people, such a big monster of a place. As usual, when she entered, the line from the Book of Job came to her mind, 'Behold now Behemoth which I made with thee.'

Before the Mass started, this being the Feast of All Saints, there was a great amount of devotion going on before the fat stone statues. The things worth looking at were the votive candles, crowds of these twinklers round every altar; Caroline added her own candle to the nearest cluster. It occurred to her that the Oratory was the sort of place which might become endeared in memory, after a long absence. She could not immediately cope with this huge full-blown environment, for it antagonized the diligence with which Caroline coped with things, bit by bit.

Having been much in Laurence's company for the fortnight past, and now alone in this company of faces, in the midst of the terrifying collective, she remembered more acutely than ever her isolation by ordeal. She was now fully conscious that she was under observation intermittently by an intruder. And presently her thoughts were away, dwelling on the new strangeness of her life, and although her eyes and ears had been following the Mass through-out, it was not until the Offertory verse that she collected her wits; *Justorum animae* . . . from sheer intelligence, the climax of the Mass approaching, she had to let her brood of sufferings go by for the time being.

'You're always bad-tempered after Mass,' Laurence observed as they cruised through the built-up areas.

'I know,' she said. 'It's one of the proofs of the Faith so far as I'm concerned. It's evidence of the truth of the Mass, don't you see? The flesh despairs.'

'Pure subjectivism,' he said. 'You're something of a Quietist, I think. And quite Manichaean. A Catharist.' He had been schooled in the detection of heresies.

'Anything else?'

'Scribe and Pharisee,' he said, 'alternately according to mood.'

'The decor of Brompton Oratory makes me ill,' she told him, as another excuse. For when he had met her after the Mass she had turned most sour.

'You don't refer to the "decor" of a church,' he said – 'at least, I think not.'

'What is it then?'

'I'm not sure of the correct term. I've never heard it called a "decor".'

'Very useful, your having been brought up a Catholic,' said Caroline. 'Converts can always rely on your kind for instruction in the non-essentials.'

Eventually, they had a clear road. Caroline pulled their spare duffle from the back seat and arranged it over her head and shoulders, so that she was secluded inside this tent, concealed from Laurence; then he guessed she was trying to suppress her irritable mood. In fact, it was getting on her nerves more and more that the eyes of an onlooker were illicitly upon them. Her determination to behave naturally in face of that situation made her more self-conscious.

Laurence was thinking about his grandmother, and as he did so he speeded up.

Two days had passed since Mrs Hogg had paid her bleak visit to Helena. Strangely, when Caroline had heard of this, she had seemed incredulous: and now, when he reverted to the subject:

'No. Helena must be mistaken. I can't conceive Mrs Hogg as a blackmailer.'

'But you've seen what she's like.'

'I don't think that particular vice is quite in her line. Opening your letter – that I do visualize. I got the impression that she's a type who acts instinctively: she'd do any evil under the guise of good. But she wouldn't engage in deliberate malice. She's too superstitious. In fact, Mrs Hogg is simply a Catholic atrocity, like the tin medals and bleeding hearts. I don't see her as a cold-blooded blackmailer. Helena must have imagined those insinuated threats.' And so Caroline rattled on, overtaken by an impulse to talk, to repeat and repeat any assertion as an alternative to absolute silence. For in such a silence Caroline kept her deepest madness, a fear void of evidence, a suspicion altogether to be distrusted. It stuck within her like something which would go neither up nor down, the shapeless notion that Mrs Hogg was somehow in league with her invisible persecutor. She would not speak of this nor give it verbal form in her mind.

Laurence could not see her face, it was behind the duffle coat. He felt exasperated by Caroline's seeming to take Mrs Hogg's part, if only that little bit.

'We've known her for twenty-odd years. We know her better than you do, dear. She's vicious.'

She snapped back at him. And so, in his need for their relations to return to a nice normal, he said peaceably,

'Yes, I suppose old Georgina means well. But she's done a lot of harm one way and another, and this time she's gone too far. We can't have Grandmother tormented at her time of life, no matter what mischief the old lady's up to. We can't, can we?' So Laurence tried to calm her testiness and engage her sympathy.

Caroline did soften down. But she surprised him when

she declared vehemently, 'I don't know that Mrs Hogg wants to torment your grandmother. I don't really think your grandmother is involved in any suspicious activity. I think you're imagining it all, on the strength of a few odd coincidences.'

It was strange. Normally, Laurence's concession, his 'Yes, I suppose old Georgina means well' should have evoked something quite agreeable from Caroline.

So he tried again. 'There's something else to be considered. That clue I got from Eleanor's cigarette case. I'm sure the crest is the same as Georgina's. There is some connection between Georgina and this Hogarth couple, I'm convinced of it.'

She did not reply.

'Strange, wasn't it, my discerning that crest, quite by chance?'

'By chance.' Caroline repeated the words on a strained pitch.

'I mean,' said Laurence obligingly, but misunderstanding her, 'that God led me to it, God bless him. Well, it's a small world. We just bump into Eleanor and –'

'Laurence,' said Caroline, 'I don't think I'm going to be much help to you at Ladylees. I've had enough holiday-making. I'll stay for a couple of days but I want to get back to London and do some work, actually. Sorry to change my mind but –'

'Go to hell,' Laurence said. 'Kindly go to hell.'

After that they stopped at a pub. When they resumed their journey Caroline began patiently to state her case. They had lost half an hour, and Laurence drove swiftly into Sussex.

'From my point of view it's clear that you are getting these ideas into your head through the influence of a novelist who is contriving some phoney plot. I can see clearly that your mind is working under the pressure of someone else's necessity, and under the suggestive power of some irresponsible writer you are allowing yourself to become an amateur sleuth in a cheap mystery piece.'

'How do you know the plot is phoney?' he said, which was rather sweet of him.

'I haven't been studying novels for three years without knowing some of the technical tricks. In this case it seems to me there's an attempt being made to organize our lives into a convenient slick plot. Is it likely that your grandmother is a gangster?'

Just ahead of them two girls in a shining black open racer skimmed the wet road. Automatically Laurence put on speed, listening intently to Caroline at the same time, for it was difficult to grasp her mind at this fantastic level.

'That's a Sunbeam Alpine,' he remarked.

'Are you listening to what I'm saying, dear?'

'I am, truly,' he said.

'Your grandmother being a gangster, it's taking things too far. She's an implausible character, don't you see?'

'She's the most plausible person I know. She'd take in anyone. That's the difficulty.'

'I mean, as a character, don't you see? She's unlikely. So is Mrs Hogg. Is it likely that the pious old cow is a blackmailer?'

'I think it likely that she's done *you* a lot of harm. She must have got properly on your nerves. She's an evil influence. You haven't been the same since you met her.'

Above the throb and tapping of the engine and the rain, he heard her, 'You don't know what you're talking about!'

'No,' he said.

'Do you really think, Laurence, that the coincidence of the crest on Eleanor's cigarette case with the one on Mrs Hogg's hairbrushes is plausible?'

'Well,' he said, 'I didn't invent the coincidence. There it was.'

'Quite,' she said.

They were losing on the Sunbeam Alpine. Laurence put on speed, so that the noise of the engine made conversation impossible. But when he had regained his ground, doing an easy fifty over the bright wet road, she asked him,

'Do you want to understand my point of view, Laurence?'

'Yes, darling, I do. Try to be reasonable.'

'It's a question of what you choose,' she said. 'If you hadn't been on the look-out for some connection between the Hogarths and poor Mrs Hogg you wouldn't have lit on that crest. And you wouldn't have been looking for it if you hadn't been influenced in that direction. I nearly fell for the trick myself, that night I stayed with the Baron. He happened to let fall a remark; it seemed to point to the suspicion that he'd been seeing your grandmother secretively during the past year, and quite often. But personally, I reject the suspicion – I refuse to have my thoughts and actions controlled by some unknown, possibly sinister being. I intend to subject him to reason. I happen to be a Christian. I happen –'

'You think the Baron's been seeing Grandmother?' Laurence pressed her. 'How did you come to think that? It's very important, dear, do tell me.'

The Sunbeam Alpine was still ahead of them. The girl at the wheel said something to her companion, who looked round. They obviously expected a race. Laurence accelerated.

'No,' Caroline said. 'That's just the point. I won't be involved in this fictional plot if I can help it. In fact, I'd like to spoil it. If I had my way I'd hold up the action of the novel. It's a duty.'

'Do tell me what the Baron said about my grandmother,' Laurence said. 'That would be the reasonable thing, my dear.'

'No, it would involve me. I intend to stand aside and see if the novel has any real form apart from this artificial plot. I happen to be a Christian.'

She said a good deal more against the plot. Laurence thought in his misery, 'She really is mad, after all. There's no help for it, Caroline is mad.' And he thought of the possibility of the long months and perhaps years ahead in which he might have to endure the sight of Caroline, his love, a mental chaos, perhaps in an asylum for months, years.

She said a great deal more about the artificial plot. Once she broke off to warn him.

'Laurence, don't try to chase those girls. They've got a supercharger.'

But he took no notice, and she continued to assure him of her resolution not to be involved in any man's story.

It was all very well for Caroline to hold out for what she wanted and what she didn't want in the way of a plot. All very well for her to resolve upon holding up the action. Easy enough for her to criticize. Laurence speeded up and touched seventy before they skidded and crashed. The Sunbeam Alpine slowed down and turned back. Laurence was still conscious, though the pain in his chest was fierce, when he saw the girls get out of their shiny racer and come towards his, where he lay entangled in his wreckage.

He saw Caroline too, her face covered with blood beside him, one of her legs bent back beneath her body most unnaturally, a sight not to be endured after he had noted her one faint moan and one twist.

PART TWO

Chapter 6

A WOMAN came in three days a week to do housework for Louisa Jepp. It was on one of these days that Mrs Hogg called at the cottage.

Mrs Jepp, keeping her on the doorstep, said,

'I cannot ask you to come inside, Mrs Hogg. My woman is all over the floors. Is it anything in particular?'

'Perhaps this afternoon,' Mrs Hogg said, and she was looking over Louisa's shoulder into the interior, right through to the green back garden.

'No. This afternoon I'm going to see my grandson in hospital. Master Laurence has had an accident. Is it anything in particular, Mrs Hogg?'

'I would like to inquire for Laurence.'

'That's kind of you. Master Laurence is progressing *and* Miss Caroline, though she's more serious. I shall say you inquired.' Louisa did not for the world suggest that Mrs Hogg might have anything further to say.

'I have a message for Laurence. That's why I came personally.'

'All the way from the North of England,' stated Louisa.

Mrs Hogg said, 'I'm here for the day. From London.'

'Come round to the back and we shall sit in the garden.'

It was a day of mild November light and sun. Louisa led the way among her pigeons across the small green patch to the bench in front of her loganberry bush.

Mrs Hogg sat down beside her, fished into her carrier bag, and pulled out an old yellow fox cape which she arranged and patted on her shoulders.

'This time of year,' she said.

Louisa thought, 'My charwoman is turned out more ladylike, and yet this woman is of good family.' She said, 'Is it anything special, your message for Master Laurence?' And while there was time she added on second thoughts,

'He is quite able to read although not sitting up yet, if you would care to write a note.'

'Oh no,' said Mrs Hogg.

Louisa thought, 'I thought not.'

'No, I shouldn't trouble him with a letter, poor Laurence, letters can cause trouble,' Mrs Hogg said. She seemed glad of the rest after the up-hill walk from the station. Observably, she gathered strength while Louisa sat beside her expressly making no reply.

'I learn,' said Mrs Hogg, 'that you call me a poisonous woman.'

'One is always learning,' Louisa said, while her black eyes made a rapid small movement in her thinking head. Mrs Hogg saw only the small hands folded on the brown lap.

'Do you not think it is time for you,' said Mrs Hogg, 'to take a reckoning of your sins and prepare for your death?'

'You spoke like that to my husband,' said Louisa. 'His death was a misery to him through your interference.'

'I nursed Mr Jepp day and night –'

'No,' said Louisa, 'only night. And then only until I discovered your talk.'

'He should have seen a priest, as I said.'

'Mrs Hogg, what is your message for Master Laurence?'

'Only that he is not to worry. I shall take no legal action against *him*. He will understand what I mean. And, Mrs Jepp,' she continued, 'you are lonely here living by yourself.'

'I am lonely by no means. I shall give no such foolish message to Master Laurence. If you have any grievance against him, I suggest you write to Sir Edwin. My grandson is not to be troubled at present.'

'There is the matter of slander. In my position my character in the world is very important.'

'You have got hold of Master Laurence's letter to Miss Caroline,' Louisa said in a voice she sometimes used when she had played a successful hand at rummy through guesswork.

'You really must remember your age,' said Mrs Hogg. 'No good carrying on as if you were in your prime.'

'I will not have you to stay with me,' Louisa said.

'You need a companion.'

'I am not feeble. I trust I shall never be so feeble as to choose you for a companion.'

'Why do you keep diamonds in the bread?'

Louisa hardly moved nor paused at all. Indeed it entered her mind: how like Laurence to have found the hiding place!

'I will not deny, that is my habit.'

'You are full of sin.'

'Crime,' said Louisa. 'I would hardly say "full". ...'

Mrs Hogg rose then, her lashless eyes screwed on Louisa's brown hands on her brown lap. Was the woman really senile, then?

'Wait. Sit down,' Louisa said, 'I should like to tell you all about the crime.' She looked up, her black old eyes open to Mrs Hogg. The appealing glance was quite convincing.

Thus encouraged, 'You must see a priest,' said Mrs Hogg. None the less, she sat down to hear Louisa's confession.

'I am in smuggling,' said Louisa. 'I shan't go into the whys and hows because of my memory, but I have a gang of my own, my dear Georgina, what do you think of that?' Louisa peered at Mrs Hogg from the corner of her eye and pursed her lips as if she were kissing the breeze. Mrs Hogg stared. Was she drunk perhaps? But at seventy-eight, after all –

'A *gang*?' said Mrs Hogg at last.

'A gang. We are four. I am the leader. The other three are gentlemen. They smuggle diamonds from abroad.'

'In loaves of bread?'

'I won't go into the ways and whats. Then I dispose of the diamonds through my contact in London.'

Mrs Hogg said, 'Your daughter doesn't know this. *If* it's true.'

'You have been to see Lady Manders, of course? You have told her what was in that letter you stole?'

'Lady Manders is very worried about you.'

'Ah yes. I will put that right. Well, let me tell you the names of the parties involved in my smuggling arrangements. If you know everything I'm sure you won't want to worry my daughter any more.'

'You can trust me,' said Mrs Hogg.

'I'm sure. There is a Mr Webster, he is a local baker. A real fine person, he doesn't go abroad himself. I had better not say what part he plays in my smuggling arrangements. Then there's a father and son – such a sad affair, the boy's a cripple but it does him so much good the trips abroad, the father too. Their name is Hogarth. Mervyn is the father and Andrew is the son. That is my gang.'

But Mrs Hogg looked in a bad way just then. The dreadful fluffy fur slipped awry on her shoulder. Violently she said, 'Mervyn and Andrew!'

'That is correct. Hogarth they call themselves.'

'You are evil,' said Mrs Hogg.

'You won't be needing that letter,' said Louisa, 'but you may keep it just the same.'

Mrs Hogg gathered her fur cape around her huge breasts, and speaking without a movement of her upper lip in a way that fascinated Louisa by its oddity, she said, 'You're an evil woman. A criminal evil old, a wicked old', and talking like that, she made off. Louisa climbed to her attic, from where she could see the railway station set in a dip of the land, and, through her father's old spyglass, Mrs Hogg eventually appeared like a shady yellow wasp on the platform.

When Louisa came downstairs, she said to her charwoman, 'That visitor I had just now.'

'Yes, Mrs Jepp?'

'She wanted to come and look after me as I'm getting so old.'

'Coo.'

Louisa opened a drawer in the kitchen dresser, took out a folded white cloth, placed it carefully at the window end of the table. She brought out her air-mail writing paper and her fountain pen and wrote a note of six lines. Next she folded the letter and laid it on the dresser while she replaced the white cloth in the drawer. She put away her fountain pen, then the writing paper, took up the note and went out into her garden. There she sat in the November mildness, uttering repeatedly and softly 'Coo, Coo-oo!' Soon a pigeon flashed out from its high loft and descended to the seat beside her. She folded the thin paper into a tiny pellet, fixed it into the band on the silver bird's leg, stroked its bill with her brown fingers, and let it go. Off it flew, in the direction of Ladle Sands.

It is possible for a man matured in religion by half a century of punctilious observance, having advanced himself in devotion the slow and exquisite way, trustfully ascending his winding stair, and, to make assurance doubly sure, supplementing his meditations by deep-breathing exercises twice daily, to go into a flat spin when faced with some trouble which does not come within a familiar category. Should this occur, it causes dismay in others. To anyone accustomed to respect the wisdom and control of a contemplative creature, the evidence of his failure to cope with a normal emergency is distressing. Only the spiritual extremists rejoice – the Devil on account of his crude triumph, and the very holy souls because they discern in such behaviour a testimony to the truth that human nature is apt to fail in spite of regular prayer and deep breathing.

But fortunately that situation rarely happens. The common instinct knows how to gauge the limits of a man's sanctity, and anyone who has earned a reputation for piety by prayer, deep breathing and one or two acceptable good works has gained this much for his trouble, that few people bring him any extraordinary problem.

That is why hardly anyone asked Sir Edwin Manders for a peculiar favour or said weird things to him.

He had coped, it was true, with the shock of the car accident; Laurence and Caroline were seen into safe hands. He floated over Helena's anxiety on the strength of his stout character. He might have managed to do something suave and comforting about Helena's other worry – her mother's suspected criminal activities. He might have turned this upset of his social tranquillity to some personal and spiritual advantage, but then he might not. Helena instinctively did not try him with this problem. She did not know what Louisa was up to, but she understood that the difficulty was not one which the Manders' cheque book could solve. Helena would not have liked to see her husband in a state of bewilderment. He went to Mass every morning, confession once a week, entertained Cardinals. He would sit, contemplating deeply, for a full hour in a silence so still you could hear a moth breathe. And Helena thought, 'No, simply no' when she tried to envisage the same Edwin grappling also with the knowledge that his mother-in-law ran a gang, kept diamonds in the bread – stolen diamonds possibly. Helena took her troubles to his brother Ernest who sailed through life wherever the fairest wind should waft him, and for whom she had always prayed so hard.

'I feel I ought not to worry Edwin about this. He has a certain sanctity. You understand, don't you, Ernest?'

'Yes, of course, dear Helena, but I'm the last person, as you know, to cope with Louisa's great gangsters. If I could invite them to lunch at my club –'

'I'm sure you could if they are my mother's associates,' Helena said.

A week later, Helena went to the flat at Queen's Gate where Caroline had lodged. It was the job of packing up the girl's possessions. Caroline's fracture would keep her in hospital for another month at least. The housekeeper, a thin ill-looking man, who, on Helena's delicate inquiries, proved not to be ill but merely a retired lightweight boxer, let her in. Nice man, she thought, telling herself that she had a way with people: Laurence and Caroline had said he was frightful.

Helena was expecting Ernest to join her. She sat for a moment on Caroline's divan; then, it was so restful, she decided to put her feet up and recline among the piled-up cushions until he should arrive. The room had been tidied up, but it was clear that Laurence and Caroline had made a sort of home of the place. The realization did not really shock Helena, it quickly startled her, it was soon over. Years ago she had come to a reckoning with the business between Laurence and Caroline and when they had parted, even while she piously rejoiced, she had felt romantically sad, wished they could be married without their incomprehensible delay. But still it was a little startling to see the evidence of what she already knew, that Laurence had been sharing the flat with Caroline, innocently but without the externals of innocence. The housekeeper had asked her, 'How are Mr and Mrs Manders? What a shame, so newly married.' Helena had kept herself collected, revealed nothing. That sort of remark – and this place with Laurence's tie over the back of the chair – caused the little startles, soon over.

'I was resting. I'm so tired running backwards and forwards to the country,' she told Ernest when he was shown up by that nice little man.

For the first few days after the accident, till Caroline was out of her long bruised sleep, Helena had stayed intermittently at a local hotel and at Ladylees with her mother. She had been watchful, had said nothing to upset the old lady. Once in the night she had turned it over in her mind to have it out with Louisa – Mother, I'm driven mad with anxiety over this accident, I can't be doing with worry on your account as well. Laurence told me . . . his idea . . . your gang . . . diamonds in the bread . . . tell me, is it true or not? What's your game . . . what's your source of income . . . ?

But supposing there was nothing in it. Seventy-eight, the old woman. Helena considered and considered between her sleeps. Suppose she has a stroke! She had refrained often from speaking her mind to Louisa in case she caused the old lady a stroke, it was an old fear of Helena's.

So she said nothing to upset her, had been more than ever alert when, on returning to the cottage one evening after her hospital visiting, Louisa told her, 'Your Mrs Hogg has been here.'

Then Helena could not conceal her anxiety.

'But I sent her away,' said Louisa, 'and I don't think I shall see her again.'

'Oh, Mother, what did she want?'

'To be my companion, dear. I am able to get about very nicely.'

'Nothing worrying you, Mother? Oh, I wish you would let us help you!'

'My!' said Louisa. 'I vow, you are all a great comfort to me, and once the children are recovered we shall all be straight with the world.'

'Well,' said Helena, 'I brought you a present from Hayward's Heath, I was so happy to see Laurence looking better.'

It was a tin-opening gadget. The old woman got out the tomato basket in which she kept a few handy tools. Helena held the machine against the scullery door while her mother screwed it in place, the old fingers manipulating the screwdriver but without a tremor.

'It's a great life if you don't weaken,' Louisa remarked as she twisted the screws in their places.

'That will be handy for you,' said Helena, 'won't it?'

'Yes, certainly,' Louisa said. 'Let's try it now.' They opened a tin of gooseberries. 'It was just what I wanted to open my cans,' said Louisa. 'You must have guessed. You have a touch of our gipsy insight in you, dear. The only thing, you don't cultivate it.'

'Now that's an exaggeration, really, Mother. Buying

you a can-opener doesn't prove anything specially psychic, now does it?'

'Not when you put it that way,' said Louisa.

Helena had already taken advantage of one of her mother's outings to search the bread bin. There were no diamonds anywhere evident, neither in the bread nor in the rice and sugar tins, nor nestling among the tea nor anywhere on the shelves of the little pantry. There Louisa also kept the sealed bottles and cans of food, neatly labelled, which she canned and bottled herself from season to season.

'Georgina wasn't horrid to you, or anything?' This was Helena's last try.

'She is not a pleasant woman by nature. I can't think why you ever took up with her. I would never have had her in my house.'

'She's had a hard life. We felt sorry for her. I don't think she can do any harm. At least ... well, I think not, do you?'

'Everyone can do harm, and do whether they mean it or not. But Mrs Hogg is not a decent woman.'

Everything stood so quiet, Helena wondered if perhaps Laurence had been mistaken, his foolish letter useless in Mrs Hogg's hands.

And that was what she told Ernest when he was shown up to Caroline's flat. She had allowed this hope to grow on her during the weeks following the accident when, sometimes alone, sometimes with her husband, she had motored back and forth between London and the country hospital. Laurence was a case of broken ribs, he could be moved home very soon. Caroline had come round, her head still bandaged, her leg now caged in its plaster and slung up on its scaffold. She had started to make a fuss about the pain, which was a good sign. Everything could have been worse.

'I doubt very much that there was anything in that suspicion of Laurence's. It caused me a lot of worry and the accident on top of it. Everything could have been worse but I'm worn out.'

'Do you know,' said Ernest, 'my dear, so am I.'

Those revelatory tones and gestures! — she watched Ernest as he picked up Caroline's blue brocade dressing-gown with the intention of folding it, helping Helena to pack, but there — before he knew what he was doing he had posed himself before the long mirror, draping the blue stuff over one hip. 'Sumptuous material!'

Helena surprised herself by the mildness of her distaste.

'The room is full of Caroline,' she remarked. 'I feel that I am seeing things through Caroline's eyes, d'you know?'

'So do I,' said he, 'now you come to mention it.'

Helena knelt by the large suitcase she had brought. Her fair skin was drawn under its frail make-up.

'We could make a pot of tea, Ernest. The meter may need a shilling.'

He put on the kettle while she considered his predicament in life. Caroline had always been able to accept his category. It was easier, Helena thought, to accept his effeminacy now that he had given up his vice and had returned to the Church, but even before that Caroline had declared, on one occasion of discussing Ernest, 'I should think God would say, "Don't dare despise My beloved freak, My homosexual."'

Helena had replied, 'Of course. But if it goes against one's very breathing to respect the man —? Oh, love is very difficult.'

'I have my own prejudices,' Caroline had said, 'so I understand yours. Ernest doesn't happen to be one of mine, that's all.'

Helena, adrift in these recollections, caught herself staring at Ernest. She lifted the phone, spoke in reply to the housekeeper's 'Yes, what number?' — 'May we have a little milk, please? We've just made some tea and we have no milk.'

Whatever he said caused Helena to exclaim when she had put down the receiver.

'Rather beastly abrupt that man! I thought him so nice before.'

She apologized for the trouble when the man brought the milk, to which he made no reply at all.

'The man's a brute, Ernest,' she said. 'He knows the sad circumstances of our being here.'

But she settled down with Ernest now, observing the peculiar turn of his wrist – he showed a lot of wrist – as he poured out their tea. Caroline with her sense of mythology would see in him a beautiful hermaphrodite, she thought, and came near to realizing this vision of Ernest herself.

'I managed to see Laurence yesterday,' Ernest said, 'remarkably well, isn't he, considering?'

'Thank God,' Helena said.

'He gave me this' – a red pocket notebook – 'and told me what he knew about your mother's friends.'

'D'you know, Ernest, I don't think there's anything to fear. I kept my eyes open those few days I spent at the cottage, but I noticed nothing suspicious. Laurence must have been mistaken, I can't help thinking. And apparently Mrs Hogg has come to the same conclusion; she actually descended on my mother while I was out. Mother was very calm about it – simply sent her away. I've no doubt – though Mother didn't say so – that Mrs Hogg came about Laurence's letter.'

'That's exactly what I should have thought. Exactly that.' Ernest was now folding Caroline's blue dressing-gown, very meticulously. 'But,' he said, 'I happen to know vaguely one of the men in Mrs Jepp's gang.'

'Oh, who's that?'

'Mervyn Hogarth. Eleanor used to be married to him. Now, *he's* most odd. Laurence thinks Mrs Hogg may be related to him.'

Helena said it was unlikely. 'I've never heard her mention the name Hogarth.' She took the notebook from him and turned its pages. The meagre dossier Laurence had prepared had a merciless look of reality. It revived Helena's fears. She was happiest when life could be reduced to metaphor, but life on its lofty literal peaks oppressed her. She peered at the stringent notes in Laurence's hand.

'What do you think of this, Ernest? Is my mother involved or not?'

'Why don't you ask her?'

'Oh, she would never say.'

Ernest said, 'Laurence thinks we should investigate. I promised him we would, in fact.'

Helena read aloud one of the unbearable pages of the notebook:

'Mervyn Hogarth: The Green House, Ladle Sands. Lives with crippled son (see Andrew Hogarth). No servants. Ex-library workshop. Bench tools. Mending (?) broken plaster statuettes. St Anthony. S. Francis. Immac. Concept. – others unrecognizable. No record in S.H. Ex Eleanor.'

'I can't make this out,' she said, 'broken plaster and the saints – are they Catholics, the Hogarths?'

'I think not,' Ernest said.

'What does "S.H." stand for?'

'Somerset House. There's apparently no record of them there. They may have been born abroad. I shall ask Eleanor, she'll know.'

'Laurence has explained all these notes to you?'

'More or less. Please don't upset yourself, Helena.'

'Oh, I did hope there was nothing more to be feared. Explain all this to me, please.'

She kept turning the pages, hoping for some small absurdity to prove the whole notion absurd that her aged mother should be involved in organized crime. She had a strong impulse to tear up the book.

'There wasn't time to go through the whole of it with Laurence. He wants me to go and stay nearby for a couple of weeks, so that I can investigate under his supervision and consult him on my daily visits.'

'No,' Helena said, 'that won't do. We can't weary Laurence in his state. I want him moved to London at the first opportunity.'

Ernest agreed. 'It would be very inconvenient for me to leave London at this time of the year. But Laurence was keen. Perhaps there's some other way –'

Helena looked at Ernest reclining now on Caroline's divan in such a hollowed-out sort of way. Shifting sand, we must not build our houses on it. But Helena was not sure whether he didn't possess some stable qualities in spite of the way the family regarded him. She realized her inexperience of Ernest: Caroline had a more lucid idea of him.

'Of course,' Helena said, 'it would cheer Laurence up tremendously, someone visiting him every day. Now that they're out of danger I can only manage twice a week. Caroline too, you would visit Caroline too?'

'I'm not sure that I can get away.'

'Ernest, I will pay your expenses of *course*.' She was almost glad of his resistance, it proved him to be ever so slightly substantial.

'If you would,' he said, 'it would be a help. But I shall have to talk to Eleanor. This time of year is difficult, and we aren't doing so well just now.'

'Please,' she said, 'don't confide in Eleanor.'

'Oh, I shouldn't mention any family business.'

They talked back and forth until it became needful to Helena that Ernest should go to reside at Hayward's Heath for two weeks.

'We must get to the bottom of this intrigue without upsetting my mother,' she declared. 'Laurence understands that perfectly. I'm sure his recovery depends on our doing something active. We must be *doing*. I know you are discreet, Ernest. I don't want Mother to have a stroke, Ernest. And we must pray.'

'I'll try to see Hogarth,' he promised. 'Maybe I can get him to meet me in London.'

He was pouring out their second cups, with that wrist,

of which there was a lot showing, poised in a woman's fashion which nibbled at Helena's trust in him.

'I have no misgivings,' she declared, 'I have implicit trust in you, Ernest.'

'Dear me,' said Ernest. She thought how Caroline with her aptitude for 'placing' people in their correct historical setting had once placed Ernest in the French Court of the seventeenth century. 'He's born out of his time,' Caroline had explained, 'that's part of his value in the present age.' Laurence had said placidly, and not long ago, 'Ernest never buys a tie, he has them made. Five-eighths of an inch wider than anyone else's.'

Parents learn a lot from their children about coping with life. It is possible for parents to be corrupted or improved by their children. Through Laurence, and also of later years through Caroline, Helena's mental organization had been recast. She was, at least, prepared for the idea that Ernest was not only to be tolerated in a spirit of what she understood as Christian charity, but valued for himself, his differences from the normal. Helena actually admired him a little for what she called his reform. But when he gave up his relations with men she had half expected an external change in Ernest; was disappointed and puzzled that his appearance and attitudes remained so infrangibly effeminate, and she understood that these mannerisms were not offensive to people like Laurence and Caroline. Helena possessed some French china, figurines of the seventeenth century which she valued, but the cherishing of Ernest while he was in her presence came hard enough to present her with an instinctive antagonism; something to overcome.

Ernest had folded while she packed nearly everything. What couldn't be packed was ready to be carried to the car. 'Let's have a cigarette, we've worked hard.'

'I suppose,' she said, 'that machine belongs to Caroline. We had better have the man up to make sure we haven't left anything of ours, or taken away what's theirs.'

Ernest, curling himself on a low footstool, lifted the

cover off the machine. 'It's a tape-recorder. Caroline probably used it for her work.'

'I have implicit trust in you, Ernest. I've come to you
before anyone. I don't want to inconvenience you of
course, and if it's a question of expense –'

'Thank you, Helena. But I can't promise – I'll try of
course – this time of year we have our bookings, our
classes. Maybe Hogarth will agree to come to London.'

'I'm so grateful to you, Ernest.'

He fiddled with the tape machine, pressed the lever. It
gave a faint whirr and the voice came with an exaggerated
soppy yak : 'Caroline, darling. . . .'

Within a few seconds Helena had recognized Laurence's
voice; a slight pause and it was followed by Caroline's.
The first speech was shocking and the second was nonsense.

Ernest said, 'Hee, silly little dears.'

Helena lifted her coat, let Ernest help her on with it.

'Will you send for the man, Ernest? Give him a pound
and ask if everything's all right. I'll take some of the
loose things down to the car. No, ten shillings will
do.'

She felt almost alone in the world, wearily unfit for the
task of understanding Laurence and Caroline. These new
shocks and new insights, this perpetual obligation on her
part to accept what it went against her to accept. . . . She
wanted a warm soft bath in her own home; she was tired
and worried and she didn't know what.

Just as she was leaving, Ernest phoning for the housekeeper said,

'Look, there's something. A notebook, that's Caroline's
I'm sure.'

A red pocket notebook was lying on the lower ledge of
the telephone table. He picked it up and handed it to
Helena.

'What a good thing you saw it. I'd quite forgotten. Caroline was asking specially for this. A notebook with shorthand notes, she asked for it.' Helena flicked it open to

make sure. Most of it was in shorthand, but on one of the pages was a list in longhand. She caught the words: 'Possible identity.'

'This must be connected with Laurence's investigations,' Helena said.

She turned again to that page while she sat in the car waiting for Ernest with the bags, but she could make nothing of it. Under 'Possible identity' were listed

> Satan
> a woman
> hermaphrodite
> a Holy Soul in Purgatory

'I don't know what,' said Helena, as she put it away carefully among Caroline's things. 'I really don't know what.'

Chapter 7

JUST after two in the mild bluish afternoon a tall straight old man entered the bookshop. He found Baron Stock alone and waiting for him.

'Ah, Mr Webster, how punctual you are, how very good of you to make the journey. Come right through to the inside, come to the inside.'

Baron Stock's large personal acquaintance – though he had few intimate friends – when they dropped in on the Baron in his Charing Cross Road bookshop were invariably greeted with this request, 'Come to the inside.' Customers, travellers and the trade were not allowed further than the large front show-place; the Baron was highly cagey about 'the inside', those shabby, comfortable, and quite harmless back premises where books and files piled and tumbled over everything except the three old armchairs and the square of worn red carpet, in the centre of which stood a foreign-looking and noisy paraffin stove. Those admitted to the inside, before they sat down and if they knew the Baron's habits, would wait while he placed a sheet of newspaper on the seat of each chair. 'It is exceedingly dusty, my dears, I never permit the cleaners to touch the inside.' When the afternoons began to draw in, the Baron would light a paraffin lamp on his desk: the electricity had long since failed here in these back premises, 'and really,' said the Baron, 'I can't have electricians coming through to the inside with their mess.' Occasionally one of his friends would say, 'It looks a simple job, I think I could fix your lights, Willi.' 'How very obliging of you.' 'Not at all, I'll do it next week.' But no one ever came next week to connect up the electricity.

'And how,' said the Baron when he had settled Mr Webster on a fresh piece of newspaper, 'is Mrs Jepp?'

Mr Webster sat erect and stiff, turning his body from the waist to answer the Baron.

'She is well I am pleased to say, but worried about her grandson I am sorry to say.'

'Yes, a nasty accident. I've known Laurence for years of course. A bad driver. But he's coming home next week, I hear.'

'Yes, he had a handsome escape. The poor young lady's leg is fractured, but she too might be worse, they tell us.'

'Poor Caroline, I've known her for years. Her forehead was cut quite open, I hear.'

'Slight abrasions, I understand, nothing serious.'

'Such a relief. I hear everything in this shop but my informants always exaggerate. They are poets on the whole or professional liars of some sort, and so one has to make allowances. I'm glad to know that Caroline's head has no permanent cavity. I've known her for years. I am going to visit her next week.'

'If you will pardon my mentioning, Baron, if you intend to be in our part of the country, I think at the moment you should not make occasion to call on Mrs Jepp. The Hogarths have had to cancel their trip to the Continent and they frequently call at the cottage.'

'What was the trouble? Why didn't they go?'

'Mrs Jepp had the feeling that the Manders were about to investigate her concerns. She thinks there should be no further trips till the spring. The Hogarths were ready to leave, but she stopped them at the last minute. She is not at all worried.'

'It sounds fairly worrying to me. The Hogarths do not suspect that I am involved in your arrangements?'

'I don't think you need fear that. Mrs Jepp and I are very careful about mentioning names. You are simply Mrs Jepp's "London connection". They have never shown further curiosity.'

'And the Manders? I suppose Laurence has put them up to something, he is so observant, it's terrifying. I am never happy when he goes to that cottage.'

'Mrs Jepp is very fond of him.'

'Why, of course. *I* am very fond of Laurence. I've known the Manders for years. But Laurence is most inquisitive. Do you think the Manders are likely to suspect my part in the affair?'

'If anything, their interest would reside in myself and the Hogarths. I do not think you need worry, Baron.'

'I will tell you why I'm anxious. There is no risk of exposure either from the Hogarths or from the Manders. In the one case they themselves are involved. In the other case the old lady is involved and the Manders would of course wish to hush up anything they found out. But it happens that I am interested in Mervyn Hogarth in another connection. I have arranged to be introduced to him, and I do not wish to confuse the two concerns.'

Mr Webster thought, 'Ah, to do with the woman, Hogarth's former wife,' but he was wrong.

'Hogarth is up in London today,' he informed the Baron, 'I saw him on the train, but I thought best to remain unseen.'

'Sure he didn't see you? No chance of his having followed you here out of curiosity?'

'No, in fact I kept *him* in sight until he disappeared into a club in Piccadilly. Ho, ho, Baron.'

He handed the Baron a small neat package. 'I had better not forget to give you this,' he said, still chuckling in an old man's way.

The Baron opened it carefully, taking out a tin marked in Louisa Jepp's clear hand, 'Soft herring roes.'

'Mrs Jepp was particularly anxious that you should eat the actual herring roes,' Mr Webster said. 'She bade me say that they are very nourishing and no contamination can possibly arise from the other contents of the tin.'

'I shall,' said the Baron, 'I shall.'

He slid the tin into his brief case, then opening a double-locked drawer took out a bundle of white notes. These he counted. He took another bunch and did likewise, then a third; from a fourth lot he extracted a number of notes which he added to the three bundles. He replaced the remainder of the notes in his drawer and relocked it before handing the bundles to Mr Webster. Then he wrote three cheques and handed them over.

'They are dated at three-weekly intervals. Please check the amount,' he said, 'and then I will give you this good strong envelope to put them in.'

'Much the safest way,' said Mr Webster as he always did, referring, not to the envelope but to the method of payment. 'Much the safest in case of inquiries,' he added as always.

When this business was done, and the notes packed into their envelope and locked away in Mr Webster's bag, the Baron said,

'Now, a cigar, Mr Webster, and a sip of Curaçao.'

'Very well, thank you. But I mustn't delay long because of the time of year.'

The shop door tinkled. 'Tinkle,' said the Baron, and rising, he peered through a chink in the partition that separated the grey-carpeted front shop from the warm and shabby inside. 'A barbarian wanting a book,' the Baron remarked as he went forth to serve his customer.

Returning within a few seconds, he said,

'Do you know anything of diabolism?'

'I've seen witchcraft practised, many times in the olden days; that was before your time, Baron; mostly in South American ports.'

'You are a sail-or,' said the Baron. 'I have always thought you were a sail-or.'

'I was a merchant seaman. I have seen witchcraft, Baron. In those countries it can be fearful, I can tell you.'

'I am interested in diabolism. In a detached way, I assure you.'

'Ho, I am sure, Baron. It isn't a thing for a temperate climate.'

'That is why,' said the Baron, 'I am interested in Mervyn Hogarth. You would call him a mild and temperate man?'

'Well, Baron, he doesn't say much though he talks a lot. Myself I don't care for him. But Mrs Jepp tolerates, she tolerates. She is thinking perhaps of the poor son. This *trading* of ours, it gives him something in life. Poor lad, poor lad.'

'Would it surprise you, Mr Webster, to know that Mervyn Hogarth is the foremost diabolist in these islands?'

'I should never have thought of the man as being foremost in anything.'

'How does he strike you, tell me?'

'Between ourselves, Baron, he strikes me, between ourselves, as a cynic, as they say, and a misanthropist. A tedious fellow.'

'Devoted to his son, though?'

'I don't know, I do not. He behaves well to the lad. Mrs Jepp believes, and this is between ourselves, Baron, that he only sticks to the boy in order to spite his former wife. At least that was her impression when she first met them.'

'This diamond trading was Mrs Jepp's idea, wasn't it?'

'Oh yes. Oh, and she enjoys it, Mrs Jepp would be the last to deny it.'

'They don't need money, the Hogarths?'

'No. Hogarth himself is comfortable. The unfortunate young man does so enjoy evading the customs, Baron.'

The Baron put a finger to his lips with a smile. Mr Webster lowered his voice as he thanked his host for the replenishment of his glass.

'Evading the customs has made a great difference to young Andrew Hogarth. It has given him confidence,' Mr Webster said in low tones.

'When Mrs Jepp first suggested this arrangement to me – for it was she, you know, who approached me with the scheme, she came straight in to the shop here a few days after I had met her with Laurence and stated her proposition most admirably; I could see her quality. Well, when she put it to me she added that if I should agree to come in with her, I must undertake not to inquire into the *methods* used by the more active agents. When I had thought over her suggestion and had satisfied myself that the plan was genuinely and well conceived – allowing for the usual risk which I do not find unpleasurable – I agreed exactly to Mrs Jepp's terms. I mention this, because frankly I would not be within my rights if I asked you by what means the Hogarths convey their valuables. Up to the past few months I have not been greatly interested in that side of the transactions, but now I am greatly inter*ested* because of my interest in the actions of Mervyn Hogarth.'

'I do not know their method,' said Mr Webster, and the Baron could not tell if he were speaking the truth or not, so unaltered were his sharp blue eyes.

'Hogarth is a diabolist. I am intensely inter*ested* in Hogarth for the reason that I am *inter*ested in the psychology of diabolism. You do not know the madness of scholarly curiosity, Mr Webster. To be interested and at the same time disinterested. . . .'

'I can well understand it, Baron. But I should not have thought the elder Mr Hogarth indulged in any exotic practices. He seems to me a disillusioned man, far from an enthusiast.'

'That is the interesting factor,' said the Baron excitedly. 'From all I have discovered of the man's personality, he is drenched in disillusionment, an intelligent man, a bored man; an unsuccessful man with women, indifferent to friendships. Yet, he is a fanatical diabolist. You will keep my confidence, Mr Webster.'

'Baron, of course. And now I must be going.'

'A fanatic,' said the Baron as he escorted Mr Webster from the inside to the outside. 'A pity the Hogarths did not go abroad. I would have called on Mrs Jepp. She may have been persuaded to tell me more of Mervyn Hogarth. However, I shall be meeting him myself very soon, I believe.'

'Good day to you, Baron.'

'My regards to Mrs Jepp.' And he added, 'Be assured, Mr Webster, the risk is neglig-ible.'

'Oh, Hogarth is not dangerous.'

'I do not mean Hogarth. I mean our happy trade. We are amateurs There is a specially protective providence for amateurs. How easily the powerful and organized professionals come to grief! They fall like Lucifer –'

'Quite so, Baron.'

'But we innocents are difficult to trip up.'

'I shouldn't call us *innocents*. Ho!' said Mr Webster stepping forth.

'That's the point. . . .' But by this time the old man had gone out of hearing.

'I don't pretend to understand women,' Mervyn Hogarth stated over the brandy. He looked at his host as if he were not sure he had said the right thing, for there was a touch of the woman, a musing effect in the baby-faced, white-haired man.

'The lamb was not right or else the sauce, I fear,' Ernest Manders mused. After all, he had not gone to Sussex. He had contrived a better plan.

'I take it you are speaking in good faith?' Mervyn Hogarth was saying.

'The lamb –?'

'No, no, the subject we were discussing, I take it –'

'Do let's take it that way, Mr Hogarth.'

'Manders, I meant no offence. I wanted to make my mind clear – only that. It seems to me a definitely odd suggestion to come from Eleanor, she knows my position, definitely.'

'It was only, you see, that we're temporarily in a tight place. Baron Stock has withdrawn his support. Naturally Eleanor thought of you. It was a kind of compliment.'

'Oh, definitely.'

'And if you can't, you can't, that is quite understood,' said Ernest.

'Have you approached your brother?'

'Yes. My brother Edwin is a mystic. He is not interested in dancing and will only invest in that which interests him. But he gave us fifty pounds. Eleanor bought a dress.'

'I can imagine Eleanor would.'

'I am myself very detached from money,' Ernest remarked, 'that is why I need so much of it. One simply doesn't notice the stuff; it slithers away.'

He sat back in his chair as if he had the whole afternoon. His guest had discovered that the business proposition for which he had been summoned was an unprofitable one.

'A quarter to three,' said Mervyn Hogarth. 'My word, the time does fly. I have one or two things to do this afternoon. People to see. Bore.'

'There *was* something else,' Ernest said, 'but if you're rushed, perhaps another time.'

'Perhaps another time' – but Mervyn Hogarth did a little exercise in his head which took no time at all, but which, had it been laboured out, would have gone like this:

Fares 13s. but had to come to London anyway; dreariness of food but it was free; disappointment at subject of discussion (Ernest had invited him to discuss 'matters of interest to you') but satisfaction about Eleanor's break with Stock and consequent money difficulties; annoyance at being touched for money but satisfaction in refusing; waste of time but now Manders wants to say something further, which might possibly redeem the meeting or on the other hand confirm it as a dead loss.

The process passed through his mind like a snap of the fingers and so, when Ernest said, 'There *was* something else, but if you're rushed –'

'Something else?' Hogarth replied.

'Perhaps another time,' Ernest said.

'Oh, I'm not rushed for the next half-hour. Do carry on.'

'Well,' said Ernest, 'it may interest you or it may not. I

feel, you know, I've brought you up to London on a dis-
appointing inducement – I did think honestly it would
please you to be substantially connected with the dancing
school – and Eleanor was sure you would – I hope you
don't feel it impertinent on our part.'

'He is like a woman,' Mervyn thought. 'It's just like
lunching with a woman.' And he assured Ernest that he
hadn't minded a bit: 'only too sorry I can't spare a penny.
What was the other question you wanted to mention?'

'Yes, well, that may be of interest and it may not. It's
just as you feel. The lamb was most peculiar, I must
apologize. It's the worst club lunch I do ever remember. I
would sent a complaint, only I did fire watching with the
chef, who is most really nice and almost never has an off
day like this.'

'A very good lunch,' said Mervyn sadly.

'*Sweet* of you to say so,' said Ernest.

'This further question –?'

'Truly you've time? I should so like to say a few words,
something which you might be interested in. You know
my brother Edwin?'

'I haven't met Sir Edwin Manders.'

'He is very rich. You know Helena?'

'His wife, that is? I know *of* her.'

'She's rather sweet. You've met her mother?'

'As a matter of fact I do know Mrs Jepp.'

'Mrs Jepp,' said Ernest.

'Fine old lady. Lives quite near my place,' said Mervyn.

'Yes, I know that,' said Ernest. 'You visit regularly, I
hear.'

'I hear,' said Mervyn, 'that her grandson had an accident.'

'Only a broken rib. He's recovering rapidly.'

'Ah, these young people. I met the grandson.'

'I know,' said Ernest.

It was creeping on three o'clock and their glasses had
been twice filled. Ernest thought he was doing rather well.

Mervyn was hoping against time, but really there was no excuse for prolonging the afternoon. Ernest had made it clear, in the soft mannerly style of pertinacity, that the Manders family had started to smell out the affairs of Louisa Jepp. Mervyn would have liked to hit Ernest for his womanly ways, and he said,

'I must say, Manders, I can't reveal any of Mrs Jepp's confidences.'

'Certainly not. Are you going abroad soon?'

'I take it this farce of asking me to lunch in order to ask me for a loan was really intended to create an opportunity to ask –'

'Oh dear, I can't possibly,' said Ernest, 'cope. I am so – am so sorry about the lunch. "Farce" is the word exactly. I do wish I had made you take duck. Most distressing, I did so think you'd be interested in Eleanor's academy, it is top-ranking absolutely if she only had the capital. How dire for you, how frightful my dear man, for me.'

'Your questions about Mrs Jepp, I can't possibly answer them,' said Mervyn, looking at his watch but unpurposed, settling into his chair, so that Ernest in his heart shook hands with himself: 'He is waiting for more questions, more clues towards how much I'm in the know.' He said to his guest, 'I mustn't keep you, then. It's been charming.'

Mervyn rose. He said, 'Look here,' and stopped.

'Yes?'

'Nothing, nothing.' But as he stood on the top doorstep taking his leave from Ernest he said, 'Tell Eleanor I shall think over her proposition. Perhaps after all I shall think it over and scrape up a little to help her out. But it's very grim these days, you realize, and I have my poor boy. He's a heavy expense.'

'Don't think of it,' said Ernest. 'Please don't dream.'

'Tell Eleanor I shall do what I can.'

For about four minutes after his guest's departure Ernest was truly puzzled by these last-minute remarks. Then he sat back in a cushiony chocolate-coloured chair and smiled all over his youthful face, which made his forehead rise in lines right up to his very white hair.

He was in Kensington within half an hour, and at the studio. He saw Eleanor in one of the dressing cubicles off the large upper dancing floor, and pirouetted beautifully to attract her attention.

She sleeked her velvet jeans over her hips, pulled the belt tight as she did always when she wanted to pull her brains together.

'How did you get on? Anything doing?'

'I think so,' he said.

'He'll put up the money?'

'I think so,' he said.

'Ernest, what charm you must have with men. I would have sworn you wouldn't get an old bit of macaroni out of Mervyn, especially seeing I'm to benefit by it. He's so mean as a rule. What did he say? How did you do it?'

'Blackmail,' Ernest said.

'How did you do it, dear?'

'I told you. It isn't certain yet, of course. And yet – I'm pretty sure you'll get the money, my dear.'

'How did you manage it?'

'Blackmail by mistake.'

'What can you mean? Tell me all.'

'I gave him lunch. I explained your difficulties. Asked for a loan. He said no. Then I asked him some other questions about something else, which he took to be a form of blackmail. Then, as he was leaving, he succumbed.'

'What questions – the ones he thought were a blackmailing effort? – What were they?'

'Sorry, can't say, my dear. Something rather private.'

'Concerning me?' said Eleanor.

'No, nothing at all to do with you, honestly.'

'Nothing honestly to do with me?'

'Honestly.'

Then she was satisfied. Ernest left her intent on her calculations, anticipating the subsidy from Mervyn Hogarth. She sat cross-legged on a curly white rug with pen and paper, adding and multiplying, as if the worries of the past had never been, as if not even yesterday had been a day of talking and thinking about bankruptcy. Before he left she said to Ernest, 'Don't forget to draw on expenses for the lunch.'

'Helena?'
'Hold the line a minute.'
'Helena?'
'Who's that? Oh, it's you, Ernest.'
'I saw Hogarth.'
'Already? Where?'
'At my club. For lunch. Frightful serious little man with a Harris-tweed jacket.'
'Ernest, you are a marvel. You will let me pay for it of course.'
'I thought you might like to know how things went. Such a glum little fellow.'
'Tell me all. I'm on edge to know.'
'Laurence is right. There is certainly something going on between your mother and Hogarth.'
'*What's* going on?'
'He wouldn't say, of course. But it's something important enough to make him most unhappy, most eager to appease us. A bleak little bodikin actually. We had such unfortunate food, lamb like tree-bark, no exaggeration. He thinks we know more than we do. That's one up for us, I feel.'
'Certainly it is. Can you come right over, Ernest? You could take a taxi.'
'It would cost ten bob.'
'Where are you speaking from?'
'South Kensington underground.'
'Oh well, come by tube if you like. But take a taxi *if* you like.'
'I'll be with you presently.'
While Ernest was telephoning to Helena that afternoon Mervyn Hogarth climbed the steps of a drab neglected

house at Chiswick. He pressed the bell. He could hear no sound, so pressed again, keeping his finger on it for a long time. Presumably out of order. Just as he was peering through the letter-box to see if anything was doing inside, the door opened so that Mervyn nearly stumbled over the threshold into the body of the blue-suited shady-looking man with no collar, who opened it.

'Is Mrs Hogg living here at present?' Mervyn said.

He was acquainted with the place, Georgina's habitual residence when in London. He had been to the place before and he did not like it.

On that day Caroline Rose in hospital heard the click of a typewriter, she heard those voices,

He was acquainted with the place, Georgina's habitual residence when in London. He had been to the place before and he did not like it.

It is not easy to dispense with Caroline Rose. At this point in the tale she is confined in a hospital bed, and no experience of hers ought to be allowed to intrude. Unfortunately she slept restlessly. She never did sleep well. And during the hours of night, rather than ring for the nurse and a sedative, she preferred to savour her private wakefulness, a luxury heightened by the profound sleeping of seven other women in the public ward. When her leg was not too distracting, Caroline among the sleepers turned her mind to the art of the novel, wondering and cogitating, those long hours, and exerting an undue, unreckoned, influence on the narrative from which she is supposed to be absent for a time.

Tap-tick-click. Caroline among the sleepers turned her mind to the art of the novel, wondering and cogitating, those long hours, and exerting an undue, unreckoned, influence on the narrative from which she is supposed to be absent for a time.

Mrs Hogg's tremendous bosom was a great embarrassment to her – not so much in the way of vanity, now that she was getting on in life – but in the circumstance that she didn't know what to do with it.

When, at the age of thirty-five she had gone to nursery-govern the Manders' boys. Edwin Manders remarked to his wife,

'Don't you think, rather buxom to have about the house?'

'Don't be disagreeable, please, Edwin. She has a fine character.'

Laurence and Giles (the elder son, killed in the war) were overjoyed at Georgina's abounding bosom. Giles was the one who produced the more poetic figures to describe it; he declared that under her blouse she kept pairs of vegetable marrows, of infant whales, St Paul's Cathedrals, goldfish bowls. Laurence's interest in Georgina's bulging frontage was more documentary. He acquired knowledge of her large stock of bust-bodices, long widths of bright pink or yellow-white materials, some hard as canvas, some more yielding in texture, from some of which dangled loops of criss-cross straps, some with eyelets for intricate tight-lacing, some with much-tried hooks and eyes. He knew exactly which one of these garments Georgina was wearing at any given time; one of them gave her four breasts, another gave her the life-jacket look which Laurence had seen in his dangerous sea-faring picture books. He knew the day when she wore her made-to-measure brassière provided at a costly expense by his mother. That was about the time Georgina was leaving to get married. The new garment was a disappointment to the children, they felt it made her look normal, only, of course, far more so. And they knew their mother was uneasy about these new shapely protrusions which did so seem to proceed heraldically far in advance of Georgina herself; the old bust-bodices were ungainly, but was this new contraption decent?

'I will lift up mine eyes to the hills,' little Giles chanted for the entertainment of the lower domestics.

The boys did not share their mother's view of Georgina's character. They were delighted when she was to leave to marry her cousin.

'What's wrong with her cousin, then?'

'Be quiet, Laurence, Miss Hogg will hear you.'

They had found her to be a sneak, a subtle tyrant. Prep school, next year, was wonderfully straightforward in comparison.

Her pale red-gold hair, round pale-blue eyes, her piglet 'flesh-coloured' face: Georgina Hogg had certain attractions at the time of her marriage. Throughout the 'tragic' years which followed (for when misfortune occurs to slightly absurd or mean-minded people it is indeed tragic for them – it falls with a thud which they don't expect, it does not excite the pity and fear of the onlooker, it excites revulsion more likely; so that the piece of bad luck which happened to Georgina Hogg was not truly tragic, only pathetic) – throughout those years since her marriage, Mrs Hogg had sought in vain for an effectual garment to harness her tremendous and increasing bosom. She spent more money than she could afford in the effort; it was like damming up the sea. By that time of her life when she met Caroline Rose at St Philumena's she had taken to wearing nothing regardless beneath her billowing blouses. 'As God made me,' she may have thought in justification, and in her newfound release.

... 'As God made me,' she may have thought in justification, and in her newfound release.

'Bad taste,' Caroline commented. 'Revolting taste.' She had, in fact, 'picked up' a good deal of the preceding passage, all about Mrs Hogg and the breasts.

'Bad taste' – typical comment of Caroline Rose. Wasn't it she in the first place who had noticed with revulsion the transparent blouse of Mrs Hogg, that time at St Philumena's? It was Caroline herself who introduced into the story the question of Mrs Hogg's bosom.

Tap-tap. It was Caroline herself who introduced into the story the question of Mrs Hogg's bosom.

Caroline Rose sighed as she lay in hospital contemplating her memory of Mrs Hogg. 'Not a real-life character,' she commented at last, 'only a gargoyle.'

Mervyn Hogarth, when he was admitted to Georgina's lodgings by the lazy dog-racing son of her landlady, was directed to Georgina's room. As he mounted the stairs towards it, he heard the swift scamper of mice, as if that part of the house was uninhabited. He knocked and jerked open the door. He saw her presently, her unfortunate smile, her colossal bust arranged more peculiarly than he had ever seen it before – and he had seen it in many extraordinary shapes – all lopsided, one side heaving up and the other one rolling down, for, possibly in the flurry of confronting him, the right shoulder strap of her bodice had snapped.

He took in her appearance without being fully aware of it, so anxious was he to speak his mind, give her warning, and be at peace.

Mrs Hogg said, collecting herself though lopsided,

'You're late, Mervyn.'

He sidled into an easy chair while she made to light the gas-ring under the kettle.

'No tea for me,' he said. 'Tell me,' he said, 'why you have started interfering. You've been to see Mrs Jepp. What's your game?'

'I know what yours is,' she said. 'Smuggling.' She sat down in her chair by the window so that the side where her bust-bodice had burst was concealed from him.

'Mrs Jepp told you that.'

'Yes, and it's true. She can afford to be truthful.'

'Andrew is involved,' he said.

'Ah yes, it's all in keeping, you have ruined Andrew already. It's only to be expected that you're making a criminal of him.'

'Why exactly did you go to Mrs Jepp?'

'I know I can do her some good if I have the chance. She's a wicked old woman. But I didn't know she had got thick with you and Andrew. When she told me "Mervyn and Andrew Hogarth" I was stabbed, stabbed to the heart.' And taking her handkerchief she stabbed each eye.

Mervyn Hogarth, looking at her, thought, 'I never pity myself. A weaker mind would be shattered by the perversity of my life. There would be plenty to pity if I were a man who indulged in self-pity.'

Georgina was speaking. 'Bigamy and now diamond smuggling. Diamond smuggling' – she repeated this crowning iniquity with dramatic contempt, upturning her profile. She looked very like Mervyn in profile.

He determined to frighten her, though he had intended only to warn.

Georgina Hogg had no need to worry about her odd appearance that afternoon, for Mervyn, though he looked straight at her, could not see her accurately. She had stirred in him, as she always did, a brew of old troubles, until he could not see Georgina for her turbulent mythical dimensions, she being the consummation of a lifetime's error, she in whom he could drown and drown if he did not frighten her.

There was no need for him to fear that the woman profiled in the window would ever denounce him openly for his bigamous marriage with Eleanor.

In their childhood he had watched his cousin Georgina's way with the other cousins – Georgina at ten, arriving at the farm for the summer holidays with her bloodless face, reddish hair, lashless eyes, her greediness, would tell the cousins,

'I can know the thoughts in your head.'

'You don't know what I'm thinking just now, Georgina.'

'Yes I do.'

'What then?'

'I shan't say. But I know because I go to school at a convent.'

There was always something in her mouth : grass – she would eat grass if there was nothing else to eat.

'Georgina, greedy guts.'

'Why did you swing the cat by its tail, poor creature, then?'

She discovered and exploited their transgressions, never told on them. She ruined their games.

'I'm to be queen of the Turks.'

'Ya Georgina lump of a girl, queen of the fairies!'

Even Mervyn, though a silent child, would mimic, 'I'm to be queen of the turkeys!'

'You stole two pennies,' and in making this retort Georgina looked as pleased as if she were eating a thick sandwich. Mervyn, the accused, was overpowered by the words, he thought perhaps they were true and eventually, as the day wore on, believed them.

He had married her in his thirty-second year instead of carving her image in stone. It was not his first mistake and her presence, half-turned to the window, dabbing each eye with her furious handkerchief, stabbed him with an unwanted knowledge of himself.

'I have it in me to be a sculptor if I find the right medium ... the right environment ... the right climate ... terrific vision of the female form if I could find the right model ... the right influences,' and by the time he was forty it became,

'I had it in me ... if only I had found the right teachers.'

By that time he had married Georgina instead of hacking out her image in stone. A *mistake*. She turned out not at all his style, her morals were as flat-chested as her form was sensuous; she conversed in acid drops while her breasts swelled with her pregnancy. He left her at the end of four months. Georgina refused to divorce him: that was the mistake of marrying a Catholic. Wouldn't let him see the son; a mistake to marry a first cousin, the child was crippled from birth, and Georgina moved him from hospitals to convents, wherever her various jobs took her. In her few letters to Mervyn, she leered at him out of her martyrdom. He sent her money, but never a message in reply.

At intervals throughout the next twenty years Georgina would put in appearances at the Manders' house in Hampstead, there to chew over her troubles. Helena hardly ever refused to see her, although she could hardly abide Georgina's presence. As the years passed, Helena would endure these sessions with her distasteful former servant, she would express banal sympathies, press small gifts into Georgina's hand and, when the woman had gone, 'offer up' the dreary interview for the Holy Souls in Purgatory. Sometimes Helena would find her a job, recommending her to individuals and institutes with an indiscriminate but desperate sense of guilt.

'I am sure you are better off without Mr Hogg,' Helena would say often when Georgina bemoaned her husband's desertion.

'It is God's will, Georgina,' Helena would say when Georgina lamented her son's deformity.

Georgina would reply, 'Yes, and better he should be a cripple than a heathen like Master Laurence.'

That was the sort of thing Helena put up with, partly out of weakness and partly strength.

One day after a long absence Georgina had arrived as of old with her rampant wounded rectitude. On this occasion she kicked the Manders' cat just as Helena entered the room. Helena pretended not to notice but sat down as usual to hear her story.

'Lady Manders,' said Georgina, dabbing her eyes, 'my son has gone.'

Helena thought at first he must be dead.

'Gone?' she said.

'Gone to live with his father,' Mrs Hogg said. 'Imagine the deception. That vile man has been seeing my boy in the hostel, behind my back. It's been going on for months, a great evil, Lady Manders. The father has money you know, and my poor boy, a good Catholic –'

'The father has taken him away?'

'Yes. Andrew has gone to live with him.'

'But surely Mr Hogg has no right. You can demand

him back. What were the authorities thinking of? I shall look into this, Georgina.'

'Andrew is of age. He went of his own free will. I wrote to him, begged him to explain or to see me. He won't, he just won't.'

'Were you not informed by the authorities before Andrew was removed?' Helena asked.

'No. It was very sudden. All in an afternoon. They say they had no power to prevent it, and I was in Bristol at the time in that temporary post. It's a shocking thing, a tragedy.'

Later Helena said to her husband,

'Poor Mrs Hogg. She had reason to be distressed about it. I wish I could like the woman, but there's something so unwholesome about her.'

'Isn't there!' he said. 'The children never cared for her, remember.'

'I wonder if her son disliked her.'

'Shouldn't be surprised.'

'Perhaps he's better off with Mr Hogg.'

'Shouldn't be surprised.'

There was only one disastrous event which Georgina Hogg omitted to tell the Manders. That was the affair of Mervyn's bigamous marriage under the assumed name 'Hogarth'.

Mrs Hogg shifted from the window to turn up the gas fire.

She said to Mervyn,

'Making a criminal out of Andrew.'

'He likes the game.'

'Bigamy,' she said, 'and now smuggling. You may get a surprise one day. I'm not going to sit by and watch you ruining Andrew.'

But he knew, she would never dissipate, in open scandal, the precious secret she held against him. He counted always and accurately on the moral blackmailer in Georgina, he had known in his childhood her predatory habits with other people's seamy secrets. Most of all she cherished those offences which were punishable by law, and for this reason she would jealously keep her prey from the attention of the law. Knowledge of a crime was safe with her, it was the criminal himself she was after, his peace of mind if she could get it. And so Mervyn had exploited her nature without fear of her disclosing to anyone his bigamy (another 'mistake' of his), far less his smuggling activities. It was now three years since Mrs Hogg had made her prize discovery of the bigamy. She had simply received an anonymous letter. It informed her that her husband, under the name of Hogarth, had undergone a form of marriage in a register office with the woman who had since shared his home. Georgina thought this very probable – too probable for her even to confide in Helena who might have made investigations, caused a public fuss.

Instead, Georgina made her own investigations. The letter, to start with: on close examination, obviously written by Andrew. She rejoiced at this token of disloyalty as much as the contents agitated her with a form of triumph.

They were true. Georgina turned up at Ladle Sands, Sussex, where the couple were established, and made a scene with Eleanor.

'You have been living with my husband for some years.'

'Quite right,' said Andrew who was present.

'I must ask you to leave,' Eleanor had kept repeating, very uncertain of her ground.

It was as banal as that.

Eleanor left Mervyn Hogg, now Hogarth, shortly after this revelation of his duplicity. She re-enacted the incident many times to the Baron. She made the most of it but her acting ability was inferior to her power of dramatic invention; what Eleanor added to the scene merely detracted from the sharp unambiguous quality of the original which lingered now only in the memories of Andrew and Georgina, exultant both, distinct though their satisfactions, and separated though they were. All the same, the Baron was impressed by Eleanor's repeated assertion, 'Mrs Hogg is a *witch*!'

Georgina wielded the bigamy in terrified triumph. Her terror lest Eleanor should take public action against the bigamist was partly mitigated by the fact that Eleanor had a reputation to keep free of scandal.

'But my name would suffer more than hers. I've always been respectable whereas she's a dancer,' Georgina declared on one of her unwelcome visits to Ladle Sands. On the strength of the bigamy she had made free of Mervyn's house.

'Moreover,' she declared, 'the affair must be kept quiet for Andrew's sake.'

'I'm not fussy,' Andrew said.

'Imagine if my friends the Manders got to hear,' Georgina said as she propped a post-card picture of the Little Flower on the mantelpiece.

For a year she made these visits frequently, until at length Mervyn threatened to give himself up to the police. 'Six to twelve months in jail would be worth it for a little peace,' he declared.

'Good idea,' said Andrew.

'You are possessed by the Devil,' his mother told him as she departed for the last time with a contemptuous glance at some broken plaster statuettes lying on a table. 'Mervyn has taken up modelling, no doubt!'

Mervyn continued to tell himself, as he sat in that room in Chiswick late in the afternoon, that if he were a man given to indulge in self-pity he would have plenty of scope. It was one mistake after another. It came to mind that on one occasion, during his matrimonial years with Eleanor, he had slipped while crossing her very polished dancing floor. Polished floors were a mistake, he had broken an eye-tooth, and in consequence, so he maintained, he had lost his sense of smell. Other calamities, other mistakes came flooding back.

It was not any disclosure of his crimes that he feared

from Georgina, he was frightened of the damage she could do to body and soul by her fanatical moral intrusiveness, so near to an utterly primitive mania.

Georgina was speaking. 'Repent and be converted, Mervyn.'

He shuddered, all hunched in the chair as he was, penetrated by the chill of danger. Georgina's lust for converts to the Faith was terrifying, for by the Faith she meant herself. He felt himself shrink to a sizable item of prey, hovering on the shores of her monstrous mouth to be masticated to a pulp and to slither unrecognizably down that abominable gully, that throat he could almost see as she smiled her smile of all-forgetting. 'Repent, Mervyn. Be converted.' And in case he should be converted perhaps chemically into an intimate cell of her great nothingness he stood up quickly and shed a snigger.

'Change your evil life,' said she. 'Get out of the clutches of Mrs Jepp.'

'You don't know what evil is,' he said defensively, 'nor the difference between right and wrong ... confuse God with the Inland Revenue and God knows what.' And he recalled at that moment several instances of Georgina's muddled morals, and he thought again of his mistakes in life, his lost art and skill, his marriages, the slippery day when he broke the eye-tooth and another occasion not long ago when he had missed his travellers' cheques after spending half an hour in Boulogne with an acquaintance of his youth whom he had happened to meet. Added to this, he had a stomach ulcer, due to all these mistakes. He thought of Ernest Manders, the hush money. He sat down again and set about to defy Georgina.

'I'll tell you what has happened thanks to your interference in my affairs. The Manders are on our trail.'

'The Manders? They dare not act. When I saw Lady Manders about my suspicions she was very very frightened about her mother.'

'You told Lady Manders? You've been busy. No wonder the affair is almost common property.'

'She was more frightened than grieved, I'm sorry to say,' Georgina said. 'She dare not act because of the mother being involved.'

'The old woman takes a very minor part in our scheme. Do you suppose we put ourselves in the hands of that senile hag?'

'She isn't senile, that one.'

'Mrs Jepp has very little to do with us. Almost nothing. The Manders are after us; they intend to make a big fuss. You see their line? – Preying on a defenceless old lady. That was the line Ernest Manders took when I met him today.'

'Ernest Manders,' Georgina said, 'you've been seeing that pervert.'

'Yes, he's blackmailing us. Thanks to your interference. But I won't be intimidated. A few years in prison wouldn't worry me after all I've been through. Andrew will get off, I daresay, on account of his condition. A special probationary home for him, I reckon. He wouldn't care a damn. Our real name would come out of course and you would be called as witness. Andrew doesn't care. Only the other day he said, "I don't care a damn".'

'You've ruined Andrew,' she declared, as she always did.

He replied: 'I was just about to take Andrew on a pilgrimage to the shrine at Einsiedeln, but we've had to cancel it thanks to your interference.'

'*You* go on a pilgrimage!' she said. 'I don't believe you would go on a holy pilgrimage, I don't believe that.'

Sir Edwin Manders had been in retreat for two weeks. 'Edwin has been in retreat for two weeks,' said Helena. Ernest, dining with her, noticed that she had said this three times since his arrival, speaking almost to herself. 'I suppose,' he thought, 'she must love him,' and he was struck by the strangeness of this love, whatever its nature might be; not that his brother was unlovable in the great magnanimous sense, but it was difficult to imagine wifely affection stretching out towards Edwin of these late years, for he had grown remote to the world though always amiable, always amiable, with a uniform amiability.

For himself, trying to approach his brother was an unendurable embarrassment. Ernest had decided that his last attempt was to remain the last.

'A temporary difficulty, Edwin. We had expensive alterations carried out at the studio. Unfortunately Eleanor has no head for business. She was under the impression that Baron Stock's financial interests in the school were secure from any personal – I mean to say any personal – you see, whereas in fact the Baron's commitments were *quite* limited, a mere form of patronage. Do you think yourself it would be a worth-*while* venture, for yourself, to satisfy your desire to promote what Eleanor and I are trying to do?' and so on.

Edwin had said, all amiable, 'To be honest now, Ernest, I have no real attraction to investing in dancing schools. But look, I'll write you a cheque. You are not to think of repayment. I am sure that is the best way to solve your problem.'

He handed Ernest the slip he had signed and folded neatly and properly. He was obviously at ease in his gesture; nothing *in* the transaction to cause reasonable resentment but Ernest was in horrible discomfort, he was unnerved, no one could know why.

Ernest began to effuse. 'I can't begin to thank you, Edwin, I can't say how pleased Eleanor ...' What he had meant to say was: 'We don't want a gift – this is a business proposition', but the very sight of his smiling brother blotted out the words.

'Why, don't think of it,' – Edwin looked surprised, as if he had written the cheque a long-forgotten twenty years ago.

Ernest fumbled the gift into his pocket and in his nervousness exaggerated his effeminate movements. Blandly the brother spoke of the ballet, of the famous dancers he had seen; this for goodwill; Ernest knew that his brother had withdrawn for many years since into a life of interior philosophy, as one might say. The arts had ceased to nourish Edwin. It was sweet of him to talk of ballet, but it put Ernest out dreadfully, and altogether he had to go home to bed. Next day he remembered the cheque, looked at it, took it to Eleanor.

'Fifty pounds! How mean! Your brother is rich enough to *invest*!' Ernest was vexed at her tone.

'Do modify your exclamation marks,' he said. 'He doesn't want to invest in the school, don't you see? He tried so hard to be nice. Fifty pounds is a generous gift.'

Eleanor bought a dress, black grosgrain with a charming backward swish which so suited her lubricious poise that Ernest felt better. With the money left over from the dress Eleanor paid down a deposit for an amber bracelet.

'Wouldn't your brother be dismayed if he knew how his sacred money was being spent?'

'No, he would not be angry at all,' Ernest said, 'not even surprised.'

For the fourth time Helena murmured,

'Edwin has been in retreat for two weeks.'

'When he returns,' Ernest said, 'you must tell him the whole story, much the best way.'

'First we shall settle the business. I never tell Edwin my troubles until they are over.'

'I feel there is nothing more to worry about. Hogarth was really scared, poor bilious little bloke he was. I pulled a gorgeous bluff.'

'If he was scared there must be something in our suspicions. Laurence was right.'

'Does it matter if we never know exactly what your mother's been doing, so long as we put an effective stop to it?'

'I should like to know a little more,' said Helena. 'But Mother is very deep, Ernest. So deep, and yet in her way so innocent. I must say I feel it a shortcoming on my part that I can't accept her innocence without wondering how it *works*. I mean, those diamonds in the bread, and where she gets her income from. It's a great defect in me, Ernest, but I'm bound to wonder, it's natural.'

'Perfectly natural, dear,' said Ernest, 'and I shouldn't reproach myself.'

'Oh *you* have nothing to reproach yourself about, Ernest dear.'

Ernest had meant to imply, 'I shouldn't reproach myself *if I were you*', but he did not correct her impression. A light rain had started to pat the windows.

'Let's employ a firm of private detectives and be done with it,' he suggested.

'Oh no, they might find out something,' she said quite seriously.

Ernest, who hated getting wet, departed soon after dinner in case the shower should turn into a steady drencher.

He had been gone nearly half an hour and it was nine-thirty, Helena thinking of saying her rosary, and of bed with a hot-water bottle since it was chilly, when the door-bell rang. Presently the middle-aged housekeeper put her head round the drawing-room door.

'Who is it, Eileen?'

'Mrs Hogg. I've sat her in the hall. She wants to see you. She said she saw the drawing-room light.' This Eileen knew Mrs Hogg; she was the one whose marriage was long ago precipitated by Laurence, his reading of her love letters. Though she had only recently returned to the Manders' service after much lively knocking about the world, she retained sufficient memory of her kitchen-girl days and especially of Mrs Hogg to resent that woman's appearances at the house, her drawing-room conferences with Lady Manders.

'I was just going to bed, Eileen. I thought an early night –'

'I'll tell her,' said Eileen, disappearing.

'No, send her up,' Helena called out.

Eileen put her head round the door again with the expression of one who demands a final clear decision.

'Send her up,' Helena said, 'but tell her I was just going to bed.'

An absurd idea came into Helena's mind while she heard the tread of footsteps ascending the stairs. She thought, 'How exhilarating it is to be myself', and the whole advantage of her personality flashed into her thoughts as if they were someone else's – her good manners and property, her good health, her niceness and her modest sense and charity; and she felt an excitement to encounter Mrs Hogg. She felt her strength; a fine disregard, freedom to take sides with her mother absolutely if necessary.

It was hardly necessary. Mrs Hogg was docile. She began by apologizing for her previous visit about Laurence's letter. 'My nerves were upset. I'd been overdoing things at St Philumena's. Some days as many as a hundred and thirty pilgrims –'

'Of course, Georgina,' Helena said.

Georgina went on to explain that she'd been thinking things over. Clearly, she had misread that letter from Master Laurence. It was all a joke, she could see that now.

'You never should have read it in the first place. It wasn't addressed to you.'

'I did it for the best,' said Mrs Hogg dabbing her eyes. And she handed the letter to Helena.

'What's this?' Helena said.

'Laurence's letter. You can see for yourself how I was misled.'

Helena tore it in two and tossed it on the fire.

'I hope you will do nothing more about it,' Georgina said.

'About what? The letter is burned. What more should I do about it?'

'I mean, about your mother. Poor old lady, I'm sure she's a holy soul,' Georgina said, adding, as she watched Helena's face, 'at heart.'

The interview continued for half an hour before

Helena realized how desperately anxious the woman was to put a stop to all investigations. It was barely a month since Mrs Hogg had descended upon her mother at the cottage. Helena was puzzled by this change of attitude and yet her suspicions were allayed by the sight of Mrs Hogg dabbing her tearful eyes.

'I'm glad you have come to your senses, Georgina.'

'I meant everything for the best, Lady Manders.'

'I understand you called to see my mother. Why was that?'

Georgina was startled. Helena was made aware of one of her suspicions being confirmed: something more than she knew had passed between her mother and Mrs Hogg.

'I thought she might want a companion,' Mrs Hogg said feebly. 'You yourself suggested it not long ago.'

Helena felt her courage surge up. 'You mean to say that you offered your services to Mrs Jepp at a time when you believed her to be a criminal?'

'A Catholic can do a lot of good amongst wicked people.'

'My mother is not a wicked person, Georgina.'

'Yes, I quite see that.'

A knock at the door, and 'Your bottle is in your bed, Lady Manders.'

'Thank you, Eileen.'

Mrs Hogg rose. She said, 'I can take it, then, that the matter is closed.'

'What on earth are you worrying about? Of course there is no more to be done,' said Helena.

'Thank God! Now I shall feel easy in my mind.'

'Where are you placed now? Have you got a job?' Helena said as if by habit.

'No, Lady Manders.'

'Have you anything in mind?'

'No. It's a worry.'

'Come and see me tomorrow at five.'

Before she went to bed Helena rang Ernest.

'Are you up, Ernest?'

'No, in bed.'

'Oh, I've woken you up, I'm sorry.'

'No, I was awake.'

'Just to say, Ernest, that Mrs Hogg came here after you left. For some reason she's highly anxious to stop all inquiries. She apologized for her suspicions.'

'Well, that's all to the good, isn't it?'

'Yes, I know. But don't you see this sudden change is rather odd, just at this time?'

'Are you sure she has nothing to do with Hogarth?' Ernest said in a more wakeful voice.

'Well, I've never heard her mention the name. Is he a Catholic?'

'Shouldn't think so.'

'Then definitely she wouldn't be *friendly* with the man in any way. She's got a religious kink.'

'You don't think she means to attempt blackmail? These blackmailers beetle round in a curious way, you know.'

'No. She actually brought me Laurence's letter. I burned it in front of her. I carried the thing off well, Ernest.'

'Of course. Well, we've nothing more to worry about from Mrs Hogg's direction.'

She was grateful for that 'we'. 'Perhaps we haven't. I told her to come and see me tomorrow about a job. I want to keep my eye on her.'

'Good idea.'

'But personally,' said Helena, 'I am beginning to think that Georgina is not all there.'

At that hour Mr Webster lay in his bed above the bakery turning over in his mind the satisfaction of the day. In spite of his tiredness on his return from London he had gone straight to Mrs Jepp, had repeated with meticulous fidelity his conversation with the Baron, and together they had reckoned up the payment and their profits as they always did.

'I am glad I sent herring roes,' Louisa said. 'I nearly sent fruit but the herring roes will be a change for Baron Stock. Herrings make brains.'

'What a day it's been!' said Mr Webster, smiling round at the walls before he took his leave.

For Baron Stock it had also been 'a day'. He hated the business of money-making, but one had to do it. The bookshop, if it had not been a luxurious adjunct to his personality, would have been a liability.

After sweet old Webster had gone, the Baron closed his bookshop for the day and, taking with him Louisa Jepp's tin of herring roes, went home. There he opened the can, and tipping the contents into a dish, surveyed the moist pale layers of embryo fish. He took a knife and lifting them one by one he daintily withdrew from between each layer a small screw of white wax paper; and when he had extracted all of these he placed the paper pellets on a saucer. These he opened when he was seated comfortably before his fire. The diamonds were enchanting, they winked their ice-hard dynamics at him as he moved over to the window to see them better.

'Blue as blue,' he said, an hour later when he sat in the back premises of a high room in Hatton Garden.

The jeweller said nothing in reply. He had one eye screwed up and the other peering through his glass at the gems, each little beauty in turn. The Baron thought afterwards, as he always did, 'I must make a new contract. This man swindles me.' But then he remembered how terse and unexcitable the jeweller was, so different from those gem-dealers who, meeting with each other on the pavements at Hatton Garden, could not contain for two seconds their business verve, nor refrain from displaying there and then their tiny precious wares, produced out of waistcoat pockets and wrapped in tissue paper. It was inconceivable that the Baron's silent dealer should ever be seen on the street; possibly he never went home, possibly had no home, but sat in vigilance and fasting from dawn to dawn, making laconic bargains with such people who arrived to sell diamonds.

Later that evening the Baron sipped Curaçao in his flat and decided that doing business was exhausting. Once every three months, this trip to Hatton Garden and the half-hearted haggle with the jeweller exhausted him. He reclined as in a hammock of his thoughts, shifting gently back and forth over the past day, and before he went to bed he began to write a letter to Louisa.

'The herring roes, my dear Mrs Jepp, have provided the most exquisite light supper for me after a most *exhausting* (but satisfying) day. I put them on toast under the grill – delicious! I admire your preservative process. The contents of your tin were more delicate than oysters, rarer than ...' But his mind drifted to other delicacies, mysterious Mervyn Hogarth, the inter-esting black arts.

What a day it had been, also, for Mervyn Hogarth, who had returned to Ladle Sands to find Andrew in one of his ugly moods. When he was in such moods Andrew would literally spit on everyone. Andrew had been left in charge of a village woman whom he had spat at so much she had gone home long before the arranged time, leaving the young cripple alone as darkness fell. When Mervyn at last got to bed he tried to read himself to sleep, but the 'mistakes' of the day started tingling; he lay in darkness fretting about the cunning of Ernest Manders, the tasteless lunch, the blackmail; and he murmured piteously to himself 'What a day, what a day', far past midnight.

And what a day for Mrs Hogg, that gargoyle, climbing to her mousy room at Chiswick where, as she opened the door, two mice scuttled one after the other swiftly down their hole beside the gas meter.

However, as soon as Mrs Hogg stepped into her room she disappeared, she simply disappeared. She had no private life whatsoever. God knows where she went in her privacy.

Chapter 8

Iᴛ is very much to be doubted if Mervyn Hogarth had ever in his life given more than a passing thought to any black art or occult science. Certainly he was innocent of prolonged interest in, let alone any practice of, diabolism, witchcraft, demonism, or such cult. Nevertheless Baron Stock believed otherwise.

It was not till the New Year that the Baron was able to assemble his evidence. He confided often in Caroline, for since her return to London they met as frequently, almost, as in earlier days. She lived now in a flat in Hampstead, quite near the Baron, with only a slight twinge in her leg before rainy weather to remind her of the fracture, and in reminding her, to bring the surprise of having had a serious accident.

'It is strange,' said the Baron, 'how Eleanor left me, her reasons. Did you ever hear?'

Caroline said, 'I know she had suspicions of your participating in Black Masses and what not.'

'I'm not surprised,' the Baron said. 'A woman of Eleanor's limited intellig-ence is incapable of distinguishing between interest in an activity and participation in it. I am interested, for instance, in relig-ion, poetr-ay, psycholog-ay, thesoph-ay, the occult, and of course demonolog-ay and diabolism, but I participate in none of them, practise none.'

'And your chief interest is diabolism,' Caroline observed.

'Oh yes, utterly my chief. As I tried to explain to Eleanor at the time, I regard these studies of mine as an adult pursuit; but to actually take part in the absurd rituals would be childish.'

'Quite,' said Caroline.

'I have, of course, attended a few Black Masses and the ceremonies of other cults, but purely as an observer.'

Caroline said, 'Um.'

It was a gusty day, and from the windows of Caroline's top-floor flat, only the sky was visible with its little hurrying clouds. It was a day when being indoors was meaningful, wasting an afternoon in superior confidences with a friend before the two-barred electric heater.

'Eleanor would not be reasoned with,' the Baron went on. 'And for some reason the idea of living with a man whose spare-time occupation was black magic appalled her. Now the curious thing is, I've since discovered that her former husband Mervyn Hogarth is a *raging* diabolist, my dear Caroline. That is obviously why she deserted him.'

'Never mind, Willi. You're as well apart from Eleanor, and she from you.'

'I've got over it. And you,' he said, 'are as well without Laurence.'

'Our case is different,' she said snappily. 'There's love saved up between Laurence and me, but no love lost between you and Eleanor.'

'No love lost,' he said, 'but still it hurts when I think of her.'

'Of course,' she said nicely.

'But not enough, my Caroline,' said he, 'to induce me to give up these investigations. People are unaccountable. One finds barbarity and superstition amongst the most unlikely. The subject, the people, excite me in-tensely. At present my attention is almost entirely on this Mervyn Hogarth. He is, I assure you, Caroline, the foremost diabolist in the kingdom. I go so far as to employ agents. I have him watched.'

'Oh, come!' Caroline said.

'Truly,' said the Baron. 'I have him watched. I get reports. I have compiled a dossier. I spend a fortune. The psychology of this man is my main occupation.'

'Dear me. You must miss Eleanor more than I thought.'

'What d'you mean?'

'Obviously your obsession with Eleanor's former lover is a kind of obsession with Eleanor. You are looking in him for something concealed in her, don't you see! Obviously you are following the man because you can't follow Eleanor, she has eluded you, don't you see? Obviously —'

'Physician, heal thyself,' said the Baron with what he thought was aptness.

'Oh, I may be wrong,' said Caroline mildly. The indoor afternoon idea went limp and she was reminded of her imprudence when, in hospital, she had begun to confide her state of mind to the Baron on the occasion of his visits. She knew he would not keep her confidences any more than she his.

But unable to leave well alone she said, 'Why really does it trouble you even if Hogarth is a diabolist? I could understand your fanaticism if you had any religion to defend. Perhaps unawares you are very religious.'

'I have no religion,' he said. 'And I don't disapprove of diabolism. For my part, it is not a moral interest; simply an intellectual passion.'

She teased him, but did not watch her words. 'You remind me of an African witch-doctor on the trail of a witch. Perhaps you picked up the spirit of the thing in the Congo — weren't you born there?' Then she saw her mistake, and the strange tinge in the whites of his eyes that had made her wonder at times if the Baron had native blood. He was extremely irritated by her remark.

'At least,' articulated he, 'I pursue an intelligible objective. Diabolism exists; the fact can be proved by the card index of any comprehensive library. Diabolism is practised: I can prove it to you if you care to accompany me to Notting Hill Gate on certain nights — unless, of course, you are too bound by the superstitious rules of your Church. Mervyn Hogarth exists. He practises diabolism; that fact is available to anyone who cares to instigate private inquiries into his conduct. You on the other hand,' he said, 'assert a number of unascertainable facts. That chorus of voices,' he said, 'who but yourself has heard them? Your theories – your speculations about the source of the noises? I think, Caroline *my* dear, that you yourself are more like a witch-doctor than I am.'

This upset Caroline, whereupon she busied herself with tea-cups, quick movements, tiny clatters of spoons and saucers. As she did this she protested nebulously.

'The evidence will be in the book itself.'

Now Caroline, one day when the Baron had visited her in hospital, had told him,

'Those voices, Willi – since I've been in hospital I have heard them. But one thing I'm convinced of' – and she indicated her leg which had swollen slightly within the plaster case so that it hurt quite a lot – 'this physical pain convinces me that I'm not wholly a fictional character. I have independent life.'

'Dear me,' said the Baron, 'were you ever in doubt of it?'

So she told him, confidentially, of her theory. He was intrigued. She warmed to the sense of conspiracy induced by the soft tones of their conversation, for it was an eight-bed ward.

'Am I also a charact-er in this mysterious book, Caroline?' he asked.

'Yes you are, Willi.'

'Is everyone a character? – Those people for instance?' He indicated the seven other beds with their occupants and visiting relatives and fuss.

'I don't know,' Caroline said. 'I only know what the voices have hinted, small crazy fragments of a novel. There may be characters I'm unaware of.'

The Baron came to see her every week-end. On each occasion they discussed Caroline's theory. And although, profoundly, she knew he was not to be trusted with a confidence, she would tell herself as he arrived and after he had gone, 'After all, he is an old friend.'

One day she informed him, 'The Typing Ghost has not recorded any lively details about this hospital ward. The reason is that the author doesn't know how to describe a hospital ward. This interlude in my life is not part of the book in consequence.' It was by making exasperating remarks like this that Caroline Rose continued to interfere with the book.

The other patients bored and irritated her. She longed to be able to suffer her physical discomforts in peace. When she experienced pain, what made it intolerable was the abrasive presence of the seven other women in the beds, their chatter and complaints, and the crowing and clucking of the administering nurses.

'The irritant that comes between us and our suffering is the hardest thing of all to suffer. If only we could have our sufferings clean,' Caroline said to the Baron.

A visiting priest on one occasion advised her to 'offer up' her sufferings for the relief of some holy soul in Purgatory.

'I do so,' Caroline declared, 'with the result that my pain is intensified, not at all alleviated. However, I continue to do so.'

'Come, come,' said the priest, youthful, blue-eyed behind his glasses, fresh from his seminary.

'That is a fact, as far as my experience goes,' said Caroline.

He looked a trifle scared, and never stopped for long at Caroline's bedside after that.

On those Saturday afternoons the Baron had seemed to bring to Caroline her more proper environment, and for the six weeks of her confinement in the country hospital she insulated herself by the phrase 'he is an old friend' against the certainty that the Baron would, without the slightest sense of betrayal, repeat and embellish her sayings and speculations for the benefit of his Charing Cross Road acquaintance. Much was the psycho-analysing of Caroline that went on in those weeks at the back of the Baron's bookshop, while she lay criticizing the book in the eight-bed ward. Which was an orthopaedic ward, rather untidy as hospital wards go, owing to the plaster casts which were lying here and there, the cages humping over the beds and the trolley at the window end on which was kept the plaster-of-Paris equipment, also a huge pair of plaster-cutting scissors like gardening shears, all of which were covered lumpily with a white sheet; and into which ward there came, at certain times, physiotherapists to exercise, exhort, and manipulate their patients.

The Baron, it is true, while he discussed 'the book' with her, had no thought for the Monday next when he should say to this one and that,

'Caroline is embroiled in a psychic allegory which she is trying to piece together while she lies with her leg in that dreary, dreary ward. I told you of her experience with the voices and the typewriter. Now she has developed the idea that these voices represent the thoughts of a disembodied novelist, if you follow, who is writing a book on his typewrite-r. Caroline is apparently a character in this book and so, my dears, am I.'

'Charming notion. She doesn't believe it literally though?'

'Quite literally. In all other respects her reason is unimpaired.'

'Caroline, of all people!'

'Oh it's absol-utely the sort of thing that happens to the logical mind. I am so fond of Caroline. I think it all very harmless. At first I thought she was on the verge of a serious disorder. But since the accident she has settled down with the fantasy, and I see no reason why she shouldn't cultivate it if it makes her happy. We are all a little mad in one or other particular.'

'Aren't we just, Willi!'

Laurence was out of hospital some weeks before Caroline.

'I can't think what possesses you,' he said, when at last he was able to see her, 'to confide in the Baron. You asked me to keep your wild ideas a secret and naturally I've been denying all the rumours. It's embarrassing for me.'

'What rumours?'

'They vary. Roughly, it goes that you've dropped Catholicism and taken up a new religion.'

'What new religion?'

'Science Fiction.'

She laughed then winced, for the least tremble hurt her leg.

'Sorry,' said Laurence who had promised not to make her laugh.

'I never expected the Baron to keep his peace on any subject,' she said. 'I rather like talking to him, it amuses me. I've been lonely here, sick as well.'

She could see that Laurence was more niggled by the Baron's attentiveness than by her actual conversations with him.

To return to that afternoon in the New Year when Caroline unwittingly hurt the Baron by comparing him to an African witch-doctor.

After tea, which she made in two pots: green for the Baron and plain Ceylon for herself, the Baron attempted to compensate for his anger. He told her a story in strictest confidence which, however, she repeated to Laurence before the day was out.

'Once, on Eleanor's behalf – shortly after her divorce from her daemonical Hogarth, and in connection with a financial settlement, I went to call on him at his house in Ladle Sands. I had not informed him previously of my intention to call, believing that if I did so he would refuse to see me. I hoped to catch him by chance – Many were such services, I assure you, Caroline, that I performed for Eleanor. Well, I called at the house. It is fairly large with some elegance of frontage, Queen Anne; set well back from the road and concealed by a semi-circle of plane trees within a high hedge that had not been trimmed for months. The garden was greatly neglected. The house was empty. Peering through the letter-box I could see a number of circular letters lying on the hall table. From this I assumed that the Hogarths had been absent for some weeks, having arranged for their personal letters to be forwarded. I went round to the back of the house. I was curious. At that time, you must understand, I was greatly in love with Eleanor, and the house where she had lived with Hogarth inter-ested me in the sense that it gave me a physical contact with a period of Eleanor's past which I knew only from what she had chosen to tell me.

'The back premises were even more untidy than the front. The kitchen garden gone to seed and stalk, and an important thing that I am going to tell you is this. At the door of an outhouse lay a pile of junk. Empty boxes, rusty broken gardening tools, old shoes. And amongst these a large number of broken plaster statuettes – religious objects of the more common kind that are sold by the thousand in the repositories attached to the Christian shrines. These were hacked about in a curious way. The heads were severed from many of them, and in some cases the whole statue had been reduced to fragments. There were far too many of these plaster pieces to be accounted for by accidental breakage. Even at that time – I knew nothing of Hogarth's occult activities then – I assumed that there had been a wholesale orgy of deliberate iconoclasm. In cases where the body was intact, only the head or limbs being severed, I noticed how cleanly the cleavage occurred, as if cut by an instrument, certainly not smashed by a fall, not that.

'Then I must tell you, Caroline, what happened while I was engaged in examining these extraordinary bits of clay. The back premises were skirted by a strip of wood-land. This was about thirty yards from the outhouse where I was standing. The sound of a dog growling caused me to turn and observe this direction, and soon I saw the dog emerge from the wood towards me. It was a black spaniel, very well cared for. I picked up a stick in case it should attack me. It approached with its horrid growling. However, it did not make straight for me. As soon as it got within five yards it started to walk round me in a circle. *It encircled me three times*, Caroline. Then it bounded towards the heap of broken statues and sat, simply sat, in front of the heap as though defying me to touch them.

'Of course I went away, walking casually in case the dog should leap. But what I am trying to tell you, Caroline, is that the black dog was Mervyn Hogarth.'

'What did you say?' said Caroline.

'I did not realize at the time,' said the Baron, stirring his green tea, 'I merely thought it an uncommonly behaved dog. Of course I am speaking to you confidentially, it is not the sort of thing one can tell one's acquaintances, however intimate. But I feel you have an understanding of such things, especially as you yourself are supernormal, clairaudient and –'

'What was that you said,' Caroline said, 'just now, about the dog?'

'The dog was Mervyn Hogarth. Magically transformed, of course. It is not unknown –'

'You're mad, Willi,' said Caroline amiably.

'Indeed,' said the Baron, 'I am not.'

'Oh, I don't mean *mad*, you know,' Caroline said. 'Just a little crazy, just a little crazy. I think of course it's a lovely tale, it has the makings of a shaggy dog.'

'I wouldn't have expected you to be incredu-lous of all people.'

'Well, Willi, I ask you!'

He was serious. 'What,' he said, 'do you make of the broken saints?'

'Maybe they had a house-full and then got fed up with them and chucked them out. Maybe they break up the statues for pleasure. After all, most of those plaster saints are atrocious artistically, one can well understand the urge.'

'For pleasure,' the Baron repeated. 'And how do you account for the dog?'

'Dogs are. One doesn't have to account for dogs. It must have been the Hogarths' dog –'

'It wasn't the Hogarths' dog. I inquired. They possess no dog.'

'It must have been a neighbour's dog. Or a stray, looking for something to eat.'

'What do you say to its having encircled me *three times*?'

'My dear Willi, I'm speechless.'

'True,' said the Baron, 'you have no answer to *that*. Not that I have formed my opinion that Hogarth is a black magician solely from the experience which I have just described to you. I haven't told you yet about the carrier-pigeons, and many subsequent phenomena. Are you free to dine with me tonight? If you are I can tell you the whole story, and then, my Caroline, you will no longer say Willi's mad.'

'We're all a little mad, Willi. That's what makes us so nice, dear. No, I'm not free tonight, I'm sorry to say. It would have been pleasant really. . . .'

He planted a friendly kiss on her cheek when he said good-bye. As soon as Caroline heard him descending in the shaky lift she went into her bathroom and taking out a bottle of Dettol poured rather a lot into a beaker of warm water. She saturated a piece of cotton wool with this strong solution; she dabbed that area on her face where the Baron had deposited his kiss.

'The Baron is crackers.'

It gave Laurence pleasure to hear Caroline say these words, for he had been lately put out by the renewed friendship between Caroline and the Baron.

'The Baron,' she declared, 'is clean gone. He came to tea this afternoon. He related the most bats tale I've ever heard.'

So she told Laurence the Baron's story. At first it

amused him. Then suddenly his mild mirth changed to a real delight. 'Good for the Baron!' he said. 'He's actually stumbled on a clue, a very important one, I feel.'

'Clue to what?' she said.

'My grandmother.'

'What has the black dog to do with your grandmother?'

'The clue is in the broken statues. Why didn't I think of it before?'

'Your grandmother wouldn't break anything whatsoever. What's the matter with you, dear man?'

'No, but Hogarth would.'

'You're as bad as the Baron,' she said, 'with your obsession about Hogarth.'

Since their motor accident Laurence had been reticent with Caroline. She saw that, because he was partly afraid, he could not keep away from her, but it was not at all to her taste to nourish the new kind of power by which she attracted him. Laurence's fear depressed her. For that reason she stopped altogether discussing with him the private mystique of her life. Only when she was taken off-guard in conversation did she reveal her mind to Laurence, as when he innocently inquired,

'How is your book going?' meaning her work on the structure of the modern novel.

'I think it is nearing the end,' she answered.

He was surprised, for only a few days since she had announced that the work was slow in progress.

Another thing had surprised him.

They had planned a holiday together abroad, to take place in the last two weeks in March.

At first Caroline had objected that this was too early in the year. Laurence, however, was fixed on this date, he had already applied for leave before consulting Caroline. She thought it rather high behaviour, too, when he announced that they would go to Lausanne.

'Lausanne in March! No fear.'

'Do trust me,' he said. 'Have I been your good friend?'

'Yes, yes, but Lausanne in March.'

'Then believe that I have my reasons. Do, please.'

She suspected that his choice of time and place was connected with his intense curiosity about his grandmother's doings. Ernest and Helena had come to believe that the danger was over. Any illicit enterprise the old woman had been engaged in was squashed by Ernest's interference and bluff. They hardly cared to think there had been any cause for anxiety. But Laurence, who had made several week-end trips to the cottage during the past winter, seemed convinced that his grandmother's adventures were still in hearty progress. Arriving unexpectedly one recent week-day evening Laurence had found her little 'gang' assembled as before, the cards in play as before, Louisa unconcerned as always. From her own lips he learned that the Hogarths had twice been abroad since January.

For his failure to pull off a dramatic swift solution of his grandmother's mystery Laurence blamed the car accident. He bitterly blamed the accident. At the same time he felt stimulated by his discovery that Ernest and Helena had between them succeeded only in putting the gang on its guard. It still remained for him to search out the old woman's craftiness. That was what he mostly desired, and not content merely to put an end to her activities, Laurence wanted to know them.

Throughout the winter his brief trips to the cottage tantalized him. He snooped round Ladylees and Ladle Sands with blank results; he had a mounting certainty that the gang was lying low. Ernest had bungled the quest. Most of all Laurence felt up against his grandmother's frankness. She was never secretive in her talk or manner, but decidedly she refrained from disclosing her secret. All he had gained was the information that the Hogarths planned a trip to Lausanne in the last two weeks of March.

'The Hogarths go abroad a great deal, Grandmother.'

'They do like travelling, my, don't they!'

He got no more out of Louisa. He applied for a fort-night's leave to start on 15 March.

Helena had been so far emancipated by her son that she saw nothing offensive in suggesting to him,

'Why not take Caroline with you? She needs a holiday and, poor girl, she can't afford one. I'll pay her expenses.'

It was then Laurence was faced with Caroline's objection, 'Lausanne in March! Why Lausanne? It will be so bleak.'

But when he said, 'Haven't I been your good friend? Do please agree with me this once,' she agreed.

That was in the middle of February. Two weeks later she disagreed.

'I've been to the Priory to see Father Jerome,' she began.

'Jolly good!' said Laurence. She had observed lately with some amusement that Laurence displayed himself keen to promote all her contacts with religion, the more as he himself continued to profess his merry scepticism. One recent Sunday when she had decided to miss church because of a sore throat, he had shown much concern, in the suggestion of a warm scarf, the providing of a gargle, and transport to and from the church in his new car, to see that she did not evade the obligation. 'Jolly good!' said Laurence, when he heard that she had visited the old monk whom he had known since his boyhood.

'He says,' Caroline announced, 'that I ought not to go to Lausanne with you.'

'But he knows me! Surely he knows we can be trusted together, that it's simply a companionable holiday. My goodness, it's done continually by the deadliest proper couples. My goodness, I always thought he was a reasonable broad-minded priest.'

'He said that in view of our past relationship, we ought not to appear in circumstances which might give rise to scandal.'

'But there's no question of sin. Even I know that. I was indoctrinated in the Catholic racket, don't forget.'

'No question of sin, but he said it would disedify,' Caroline said.

'We needn't tell anyone we're going together. And we're hardly likely to be seen by anyone at all in Lausanne in March.'

'A furtive trip would be worse than an open one. More disedifying still. I can't go. Awfully sorry.'

Her withdrawal upset Laurence more than she expected. He had not told her that, as she had guessed, his determination to visit Lausanne in March was in some way connected with his passion to play the sleuth on his grandmother. She had not reckoned with his need for her participation, and the more he argued with her the more she conceived herself well out of the affair. It reminded her too much of the pattern of events preceding the car-smash.

Laurence did not press her very far. He accepted her decision with that strange fear he now had of approaching close enough to Caroline to precipitate a row. It was on this occasion that, suppressing his disappointedness, he asked her amicably,

'How is your book going?' and she, her mind brooding elsewhere, answered, 'I think it is nearing the end.'

'Really? You were saying only the other day that you still had a lot to write.'

Swiftly she realized her mistake, and so did Laurence. He looked rather helpless, as if enmeshed. She hated to think of herself as a spiritual tyrant, she longed to free him from those complex familiars of her thoughts which were to him so foreign.

'Naturally, I look forward to the end of the book,' she said, 'in a manner of speaking to get some peace.'

'I meant,' said Laurence with a burst of irritation, 'of course, the book that you are writing, not the "book" in which you think you are participating.'

'I know,' she said meekly, 'that is what you meant.' And to lift the heavy feeling between them she gave him her pretty, civilized smile and said, 'Do you remember

170

that passage in Proust where he discusses the ambiguous use of the word "book", and he says –?'

'To hell with Proust,' said Laurence.

'Look,' she said, 'I don't inquire into your fantastic affairs. Leave mine alone. And look,' she said, 'we have nothing to say to each other this evening. I'm going home. I'll walk.'

They were dining in a small restaurant only a few minutes' walk from Caroline's flat, and so her 'I'll walk', falling short of its intended direness, tickled Laurence.

'I find it difficult to keep up with you these days.' And to pacify her he added, 'Why do you say that the "book" is nearing the end?'

She was reluctant to answer, but his manner obliged her.

'Because of incidents which have been happening within our orbit of consciousness, and their sequence. Especially this news about your grandmother's friend.'

'Which friend?' said Laurence.

'Haven't you heard about it? Helena rang me this morning, very excited, and from what I can gather it's most remarkable –'

'Which friend?'

'One of those concerning whom you entertain your daft suspicions. Andrew Hogarth. Apparently he was paralysed, and his father took him off to some little shrine of Our Lady in the French Alps. Well, he was brought back yesterday and he's actually started to move his paralysed limb. Helena says it's a miracle. I don't know about that but it seems the sort of incident which winds up a plot and brings a book to a close. I shan't be sorry.'

'But they haven't been abroad since January. They hadn't planned to leave until the middle of March, at least so I understood. I have reason to believe the Hogarths are diamond smugglers, don't you understand?'

'Ask your mother,' Caroline said. 'She knows all about it. She's brimming full of it.'

'I don't see,' said Laurence, 'much point, now, in going to Lausanne in March.'

'Absolutely perfect ... A pass back there – a foul tackle and the whistle ... the sun has come out, everything looks *absolutely perfect* with the red coats of the band ... that feeling of – of tenseness ... and now again for the second half ... the first dramatic ... absolutely perfect ... it's a *corner*, a goal to Manchester City ... a beautiful, absolutely...'

Louisa Jepp sat beside the wireless cuddled in the entranced carcass of Laurence's voice.

Much later in the day, after he had braked up loudly outside the cottage in his new car, and had settled into a chair by the stove with a newly-opened bottle of beer, he said,

'Is it true about young Hogarth?'

'He is receiving physiotherapeutic treatment,' she said, with correctness, for she used and pronounced her words, however unlikely, accurately, or not at all.

'And he has actually started to use his legs?'

'Yes. He totters a little. It's too soon to say "he walks".'

'He was absolutely paralysed before.'

'My, yes. The trips abroad did him good. I always knew they would.'

'I suppose,' said Laurence, 'that the Hogarths have cancelled their holiday in Lausanne?'

'Oh yes. There's no need for them to go wandering in March. It's very chilly. Much better at home. Andrew is getting his treatment.'

'I suppose,' said Laurence, 'they will be off again in the early summer?'

'Not abroad,' said the old lady. 'Somerset or Cornwall I should say, if the boy's fit enough.'

'I suppose that means,' said Laurence, 'that your game is up, Grandmother?'

'Why, dear,' she said, 'I was thinking, as I listened to you on the wireless today, how much I wished for your sake, dear, that you could have caught us red-handed. It must be a disappointment, love. But never mind, we all have our frustrations and you were lovely on the wireless, you were *absolutely perfect*.'

'I had every clue, Grandmother. I only needed the time. If I hadn't had the smash I'd have got you last autumn, Grandmother.'

'There, never mind.'

'But you're in danger. An acquaintance of ours is on your trail. I heard by chance through Caroline. His name's Willi Stock, a phoney Baron –'

'No, he is quite authentic a Baron.'

'You know Baron Stock, then?'

'I have met the Baron,' she said.

'Well, do you know,' he said, 'Caroline told me last November, just before the smash, that the Baron had been seeing you last year. He described a hat you wore. Caroline recognized it, and inferred –'

'That was very stupid of the Baron, but typical, though he is nice –'

'But I didn't,' said Laurence, 'place much faith in what Caroline said. I thought she was sort of dreaming.'

'Why, you can't be clever at everything.'

'It was a good clue,' said Laurence. 'I ought to have followed it up. I might have got you right away. Have you any fears of the Baron? – Because if so –'

'No, no. He's my London party. Or was.'

'The *Baron* has been in with you! I thought there were only the four of you.'

'There are only four of us. Baron Stock was only our London agent.'

'You've packed up the game, then?'

'Now, which game?' she said, puckering a smile as if to encourage him to recite a lesson.

'Smuggling diamonds through the customs,' he said, 'concealed in plaster figures.'

'And rosary beads at times,' said Louisa. Her whole body seemed to perk with delight, and to further signify her sense of occasion she passed Laurence a glass and a bottle of stout to open for her. She watched him pour the brown liquid and she watched the high self-controlled froth as one who watches a scene to be preserved in memory.

'You took a risk, Grandmother.'

'There was very small risk,' she said. 'What there was, the Hogarths took, as I see it.'

She drew up to the stove and sipped warmly.

'I had many a smile,' she said, 'considering how they came through with the merchandise.'

'Several times a year,' said Laurence, 'at a guess.'

'It has varied,' she said, 'over four years and eight months. Some trips were better than others. It depended so much on our continental parties. It was difficult for that end to get the right moulds for the statues. The beads were easier. But Andrew preferred the statues.'

'I should have thought the customs would have got suspicious with all that coming and going. Very risky,' Laurence said.

'Everything's risky,' she said. 'Many a laugh I had to myself when Mervyn told me about the customs men passing remarks. *Mervyn* didn't laugh, he didn't like that part of it. You see they went as pilgrims looking for a cure, Andrew in his invalid chair, you can picture him, hugging his statues with a long churchy face. So as to deceive the customs, don't you see. Each time they went to some shrine of the Virgin Mary and our contact would meet them in the town, who was a gentlemanly party I believe. But I made Mervyn and Andrew visit the shrines properly, in case they were watched. You can't be too careful with the continental police, they are very deceitful and low.'

'Are the Hogarths Catholics?'

'Oh, no. Not religious at all. That was the pose, you see. Many an entertainment I had, love.'

'Mother has heard about Andrew Hogarth's recovery,' Laurence said.

'Yes, I wrote and told her. I thought it would be of interest to her that the young man, being a neighbour of mine, had got a cure at a Roman Catholic shrine. She likes those stories.'

'Do you think it was a miracle, then?'

'Oh yes,' she said, 'I do believe in lucky places if your luck is in. Indeed Andrew was unlucky before. He got a cold in the bladder at Lourdes two years back, but Myans has brought him luck, where there's a *black* Madonna, I believe. And indeed I once knew a gentleman very up in history and fond of the olden days who had a stammer which he lost in the Tower of London.'

'That sounds psychological,' said Laurence.

'Oh, it's all what I call luck,' Louisa said.

'You don't think Andrew's case is clearly a miracle, then?'

'Oh, quite clear a miracle, as I see him now. He can move his legs from the knees, sitting in his chair. He couldn't do that before.'

'What do the doctors say?'

'They say he has to have physiotherapy. He's improving already.'

'How do they explain it?'

'They say it's a marvel but they don't make mention of miracles. They brought a great crowd of students to look at Andrew up at the hospital. Andrew put an end to it, though, by swearing and spitting. He has such a temper.'

'Good for him!' Laurence said. 'I suppose he's thrilled to be able to move his legs?'

'I think so. But he has a temper,' she said, and passing a box of cigarettes, 'Have a Bulgarian.'

Laurence smiled, comparing this account of Andrew with the picture in his mother's imagination of the young man miraculously cured. In Helena's eyes, the event entirely justified the Hogarths' shady activities. It justified her mother. She was content to remain vague about Louisa's late intrigues, and convinced that Ernest, through his strong hand with Mervyn Hogarth last year in the course of a luncheon, had been successful in ending the troubles, whatever they were.

When she told Laurence of Andrew's cure at the Alpine shrine, he remarked,

'They're still at the game, then.'

'Nonsense,' Helena replied. 'At the very worst, the Hogarths might have been winding up their business, whatever it was. I expect they will both become Catholics. The young man will, surely.'

'Helena wants to make a Church thing of it,' Louisa told Laurence. 'But she won't be able to. I'm sorry for her sake, but the Hogarths aren't interested at all in churches.'

'Like me,' said Laurence.

'No, not at all. They aren't interested in quite a different way from you.'

The old woman had sipped from her glass only at long intervals. Even so, Laurence was fascinated to notice how little she had drunk, while giving the companionable appearance of keeping pace with him.

'I suppose,' he said, 'you made a packet between you.'

'Yes. I meant to retire this year in any case.'

Helena had developed a firm new theory about her mother's motives. 'I am sure she involved herself in all that unpleasantness, whatever it was, simply to help the young man. My mother is extremely secretive. She is quite capable of *planning* to send him to the holy shrines, using the financial reward as a bribery.'

Laurence reported this to his grandmother. She wrinkled her nose and sipped from her glass. 'Of course I knew the trips would be good for Andrew. Psychologically. It gave him a job to do and a change now and then. The business side was good for me too. Psychologically. I shall miss it, dear, it was sport. Helena is sentimental, my!'

'What was Mr Webster's role, Grandmother?'

'Oh, the good fellow baked the bread, and he sometimes went to London for me.'

'Now tell me where the bread comes in,' said Laurence.

'You found diamonds in the bread, and you wrote to

176

tell Caroline of it. That caused a lot of trouble.' – Laurence, feeling sleepy from his day's work, the warmth and the beer, was not quite sure whether he heard or imagined these words.

'What did you say, Grandmother?'

The glass was at her lips. 'Nothing, dear,' she said when she had sipped.

'Tell me about the bread. Who transferred the diamonds to the bread? You know I saw them once.'

'Mr Webster,' she said. 'Because I desired to have my merchandise quickly, as soon as the Hogarths brought it in. For the sake of the London end. Sometimes, at first, there was a little delay owing to Andrew being poorly after the journey and leading Mervyn a dance. So we arranged that Mervyn should break up his saints and rosaries and extract the stones as soon as he returned from the trips, which was always in the morning. Mervyn would telephone Mr Webster, because they use telephones, I stick to my pigeons. And then Mr Webster called at the Hogarths to deliver the bread.'

'Ostensibly,' said Laurence.

Louisa closed her eyes. 'He called to deliver the bread as it might seem. You can't be too careful. And he took the money for it.'

'Along with the diamonds.'

'Yes, you are clever, dear. Mr Webster has been invaluable. He would bring the merchandise to me on the following morning in my bread. I didn't think it would be nice to let him slip the little goods into my hand as if there were some mystery or anything shady going on.'

'Wonderfully ingenious,' Laurence said.

'It was sport,' said Louisa.

'But totally unnecessary, the bread part of it,' Laurence said.

'No, that was necessary. I never liked to have the diamonds carried loose.'

'I can guess why,' Laurence put in suddenly. 'The police.'

'Of course,' she said. 'I don't trust the police. Our local constable is a nice fellow, but the police all stick together if it comes to the bit, the world over.'

Laurence laughed. Louisa's dislike of the police was a family joke. 'It's the gipsy in her,' Helena would explain.

'I should have thought,' Laurence said, 'that if you got the goods safely into the country, there would be no need for elaborate precautions.'

'You never can tell. It was sport,' Louisa said.

After a while Laurence said, 'I believe Mrs Hogg gave you some trouble.'

'None at all,' she said, 'nor will she.'

'You think she's likely to turn up again? Has she any evidence against you, Grandmother?'

'I don't know about that. But she won't trouble me, that I know. She might try, but I shan't be troubled.' She added, 'There are things about Mrs Hogg which you don't know.'

At a later time when Laurence learned of the relationship between Mrs Hogg and the Hogarths, he recalled this remark of his grandmother's, and thought that was what she must have meant.

'And at a side altar, I do assure you, Caroline,' said the Baron, 'robed in full liturgical vestments, was Mervyn Hogg alias Hogarth serving cocktails.' Thus he ended his description of the Black Mass he had recently attended at Notting Hill Gate.

'It sounds puerile,' Caroline said, lapsing unawares into that Catholic habit of belittling what was secretly feared.

'You as a Catholic,' he said, 'must think it evil. I myself do not judge good and evil. I judge by interesting or otherwise.'

'It sounds otherwise to me,' said Caroline.

'In fact you are right. This was a poor effort from the sinister point of view. For a really effective Black Mass you need a renegade priest. They are rare in these days, when the Faith is so thin. But Hogg is the one who inter*ests* me. He assumes the name of Hogg on the dark side of his life and Hogarth by daylight so to speak. I am preparing a monograph on the psychology of diabolism and black magic.

'And my informants tell me that Hogarth has recently un-bewitched his son, a man in his early twenties who since infancy has suffered from paralysis in the lower part of his body due to a spell. This proves that Hogarth's magical powers are not exclusively bent towards evil, it proves –'

'Tell me,' said Caroline, 'have you ever spoken to Mervyn Hogarth?'

'Not in his natural flesh. But I shall shortly. A private meeting is to be arranged. Unofficially, I believe, he has been into the bookshop, transformed into a woman.'

'I'm sure, Willi,' said Caroline, 'that you are suffering from the emotional effects of Eleanor's leaving you. I am sure, Willi, that you should see a psychiatrist.'

'If what you say were true,' he said, 'it would be horribly tactless of you to say it. As it is I make allowances for your own disorder.'

'Is the world a lunatic asylum then? Are we all courteous maniacs discreetly making allowances for everyone else's derangement?'

'Largely,' said the Baron.

'I resist the proposition,' Caroline said.

'That is an intolerant attitude.'

'It's the only alternative to demonstrating the proposition,' Caroline said.

'I don't know,' said the Baron, 'really why I continue to open my mind to you.'

At various times the Baron had described to Caroline the stages by which he had reached the conclusion that Mervyn Hogarth was a diabolist and magician. The first hint had come to him from Eleanor. 'She told me he had previously been through a form of marriage with a witch. Eleanor had seen the witch, a repulsive woman. In fact, it was when she began to frequent the house in Ladle Sands that Eleanor left Hogarth.'

'I shouldn't take much account of what Eleanor says. She dramatizes a lot,' said Caroline, and barely refrained from adding the information that Eleanor, in her college days, had been wont to send love-letters to herself. Caroline only refrained because she was not too sure if this were true.

'My subsequent experience has borne out her allegations. My subsequent investigations have proved that Hogarth is the foremost diabolist in the kingdom. One must speak as one experiences and as one finds. You, Caroline, are no exception. Your peculiar experiences are less explicable than mine: I have the evidence. The broken plaster images: a well-known diabolic practice: the black dog. If you would only enter*tain* the subject a little more you would see that I am right.'

So he attempted to extort sympathy from Caroline. He appeared to her more and more in the nature of a demanding creditor. 'The result,' she told herself, 'of going to him with my troubles last autumn. He acted the old friend and now he wants me to do the same, which is impossible.'

And she told him, 'You are asking me to entertain impossible beliefs: what you claim may be true or not; I have doubts, I can't give assent to them. For my own experiences, however, I don't demand anyone's belief. You may call them delusions for all I care. I have merely registered my findings.'

Caroline had been reflecting recently on the case of Laurence and his fantastic belief that his grandmother had for years been the leader of a gang of diamond-smugglers. She had considered, also, the case of the Baron and his fantastic belief in the magical powers of Mervyn Hogarth. The Baron was beginning to show a sickly resemblance to Eleanor. She thought of Eleanor with her habit of giving spontaneous utterance to stray and irresponsible accusations. Caroline found the true facts everywhere beclouded. She was aware that the book in which she was involved was still in progress. Now, when she speculated on the story, she did so privately, noting the facts as they accumulated. By now, she possessed a large number of notes, transcribed from the voices, and these she studied carefully. Her sense of being written into the novel was painful. Of her constant influence on its course she remained unaware and now she was impatient for the story to come to an end, knowing that the narrative could never become coherent to her until she was at last outside it, and at the same time consummately inside it.

Eventually she told the Baron that she simply wasn't interested in black magic. She forbade the subject.

'It gets on my nerves, Willi. I have no sympathy with your occult interests. Talk about something else in future.'

'You are lost,' he said sadly, 'to the world of ideas. You had the makings of an inter-esting mind, I do assure you, Caroline. Ah, well!'

One morning Caroline had an unexpected caller. She had opened the door of her flat unguardedly, expecting the parcel post. For a second Caroline got the impression that nobody was there, but then immediately she saw the woman standing heavily in the doorway and recognized the indecent smile of Mrs Hogg just as she had last seen it at St Philumena's.

'May I have a word with you, Miss Rose?' Already the woman was in the small square hall, taking up most of it.

'I'm busy,' Caroline said. 'I work in the mornings. Is it anything urgent?'

Mrs Hogg glared with her little eyes. 'It's important,' she said.

'Will you come inside, then?'

She seated herself in Caroline's own chair and cast her eyes on the notebook in which Caroline had been writing. It was lying on a side table. Caroline leant forward and snapped the book shut.

'There is a Baron Stock,' said Mrs Hogg. 'He was in your flat till after one o'clock this morning. He was in your flat till after two on Wednesday morning. You were in his flat till after midnight twice the week before last. If you think you are going to catch Laurence Manders with this carry-on –'

'You are insolent,' Caroline said. 'You'll have to leave.'

'Till after two on Wednesday morning. Baron Stock is more attractive than Laurence Manders, I don't doubt, but I think it low behaviour and so would everyone –'

'Take yourself off,' said Caroline.

She left, pathetic and lumpy as a public response. Caroline seized the phone angrily and rang Helena.

'Would you mind calling off your Mrs Hogg. She's just been round here making wild insinuations about my private life, citing Willi Stock. She must have been watching my flat for weeks. Haven't you any control over the woman? I do think, Helena, you are far too soft with that woman. She's a beast. If there's any more trouble I shall simply call the police, tell her that.'

'Dear me. I haven't seen Mrs Hogg for months. I *am* sorry, Caroline. Won't you come round to lunch? I recommended Mrs Hogg for a job in a place at Streatham last autumn. I haven't heard from her since. We've got a new sort of risotto, quite simple, and heaps to spare. Edwin won't be in to lunch. Have you seen Laurence lately?'

'You ought not to recommend Mrs Hogg for jobs. She's quite vile.'

'Oh, one tries to be charitable. I shall speak severely. Did she upset you seriously, Caroline?'

'No, she did not. I mean, she did, yes. But it's not what she says, it's what she is.'

'She's not all there,' said Helena.

Presently, Caroline sprayed the room with a preparation for eliminating germs and insects.

Chapter 9

'WONDERFUL to have a whole day unplanned,' Caroline said. 'It's like a blank sheet of paper to be filled in according to inspiration.'

It was summer, on a day which Laurence described as absolutely perfect for a riverside picnic. They chose their spot and got the luncheon boxes out of the car. It was Laurence's day off. Helena too had decided to have a day off.

'I've been working so hard on the committees, and Edwin is in retreat – I should love a day in the country,' she admitted when Laurence invited her to join them. 'But I hate intruding. You and Caroline enjoy yourselves together, do.'

But she yielded easily when Caroline too insisted on her coming.

'All right. But you two go ahead. I'll join you before lunch, if you tell me where to find you.'

They described the area where they intended to park, on the banks of the Medway where it borders Kent and Sussex.

There they were at midday sunning themselves lusciously and keeping an intermittent look-out for Helena's car.

She arrived at half past twelve, and they could see as she bumped down the track towards them that she had brought two people with her, a man beside her in the front and a woman with a black hat at the back.

The couple turned out to be the Baron and Mrs Hogg.

Helena, uncertain of her welcome, and unusually nervous, began immediately,

'Such fun. Willi phoned me just after you'd left and d'you know what, he's been meaning to come down here the first opportunity. He wants to look at an Abbey in these parts, don't you, Willi? So I made him come. And I've brought poor Mrs Hogg, I made her come. It was a lovely ride, wasn't it? Poor Georgina's had neuralgia. She called round to the house by chance just after you'd left, so I made her come. A day in the country will do you a world of good, Georgina. We shan't interfere with your plans, Laurence. We've brought extra lunch and you can go off by yourselves if you like while we sit in the sun.'

Helena looked a trifle shaky. While they prepared lunch she made the opportunity of a private word with Caroline,

'I hope you don't mind dreadfully, dear, about my bringing Georgina. She turned up so desolate, and there was I so obviously preparing the picnic basket. I asked her on impulse and of course she jumped to it – I was rather sorry afterwards, remembering how much you dislike her. Do try to ignore her and if she says anything funny to you just shake her off. I know how you feel about Georgina for I can't bear the sight of her at times, but one tries to be charitable.'

'Don't you think,' Caroline said, 'that you misconstrue charity?'

'Well, charity,' said Helena, 'begins at home. And Georgina *has* been part of our household.'

'Mrs Hogg is not home,' Caroline said.

'Oh dear, I wish I hadn't asked her to come. It was foolish of me, I've spoiled your day.'

'The day isn't over yet,' said Caroline cordially, for the weather was glorious really.

'But still I wish I hadn't brought her, for another reason. Something happened on the way here, Caroline. It was disturbing.' Caroline saw she was distressed.

'Come over here and help me to take out the bottles,' Caroline said, 'and tell me what happened.'

'I gave Georgina a tablet for her neuralgia before we set off,' Helena said, 'and sat her comfortably at the back of the car. Before we were out of London I said over my shoulder, "Are you all right, Georgina?" She replied that she was feeling sleepy. I went on chatting to Willi and thought no more of Georgina at the back. I assumed she had fallen asleep for I could hear her breathing rather heavily.'

'She snores,' Caroline said. 'I remember at St Philumena's I could hear her snoring six doors away.'

'Well, yes, she was snoring,' Helena said. 'And I thought the sleep would do her good. After a while she stopped snoring. I said to Willi, "She's dead asleep." Then Willi's cigarette lighter gave out and he asked for some matches. I thought there were some at the back of the car, but I didn't want to wake Georgina. So I pulled up. And when I turned to reach for the matches, I couldn't see Georgina.'

'Why, what had happened?'

'She simply wasn't there,' Helena declared. 'I said to Willi, "Heavens, where's Georgina?" and Willi said, "My God! she's gone!" Well, just as he said this, we saw Georgina again. She suddenly appeared before our eyes at the back of the car, sitting in the same position and blinking, as if she'd just then woken up. It was as if there'd been a black-out at the films. I would have thought I'd been dreaming the incident, but Willi apparently had the same experience. He said, "Where have you been, Mrs Hogg? You vanished, didn't you?" She looked really surprised, she said, "I've been asleep, sir." '

'It may have been some telepathic illusion shared by you and Willi,' Caroline said. 'I shouldn't worry.'

'Maybe it was. I haven't had an opportunity to discuss this privately with Willi. It was a most strange affair; truly I wish I hadn't brought Georgina. Sometimes I feel I can handle her, but at other times she seems to get the better of me.'

'Maybe when she goes to sleep she disappears as a matter of course,' Caroline said with a dry laugh so that Helena would not take her too seriously.

'What a gruesome idea. Well, I swear that she did apparently vanish. All I saw when I first looked round was the empty seat.'

'Maybe she has no private life whatsoever,' Caroline said, and she giggled to take the grim edge off her words.

'Oh, she has no private life, poor soul,' Helena agreed, meaning that the woman had no friends.

Mrs Hogg ate heartily at lunch. Caroline sat as far away from her as possible to avoid the sight of her large mouth chewing, and the memory of that sight when, at St Philumena's, she had first observed Mrs Hogg sitting opposite to her at the refectory table, chew – pause – chew – pause. Mrs Hogg spoke little, but she was very much present.

After lunch, Caroline was stacking an empty food box in the boot of Helena's car some distance from the rest of the party, when the Baron approached her.

'Summer suits you, my Caroline,' he said. 'Your sun dress is charming. Green suits you, and you are plumper. I thought you a delightful picture at lunch, so secluded within your proud personality as you always seem to be and with such a watchful air.'

Caroline appreciated flattery, the more so when it was plainly excessive and well laid on, for then she felt that the flatterer had really taken pains to please. So she smiled languidly and waited for the rest, not at all surprised that these remarks were a prelude to one of those 'confidences' which the Baron so greatly longed to make. For, since she had forbidden the subject of black magic, the Baron had been manifestly unhappy. She realized that he had chosen her as a repository for his secret enthusiasm because of that very edginess and snap with which she responded. If, like his other friends, she could have been merely sociable about his esoteric interests, making a gay palaver of them – 'Do describe the formula, Willi, for changing oneself into a fly. One could watch all one's friends. . . . Suppose one got stuck in a pot of jam' – if only she could have played buoyant and easy with the Baron, he never would have plagued her with his 'confidences'.

Having lubricated the way with his opening speech he proceeded instantly,

'I must tell you, Caroline, such a strange thing happened in the car as we came down. This woman, Mrs Hogg –'

Caroline tried to be pleasant. 'Helena has already told me of the incident. Obviously, Willi, you've been infecting Helena with your fancies. Obviously –'

'I do assure you, Caroline, I have never discussed any occult subject with Helena. I am very careful in whom I confide these matters. There is no other way of accounting for the strange phenomenon in the car but to accept the fact that this woman Hogg is a witch.'

'Not necessarily,' Caroline said, 'even if she did disappear. I think she's too ignorant to be a witch.' And she added, 'Not that I believe in witches particularly.'

'And I have made a curious discovery,' the Baron continued relentlessly. 'Don't you see – this woman Hogg is, I am certain, the witch to whom Mervyn Hogarth was married. The facts meet together – he *has* been known to use the name Hogg, as I told you. My informants say he always used it in his younger days. This Georgina Hogg is his witch-wife.'

'Nonsense. She's an old servant of the Manders. I believe she married a cousin. She has a crippled son somewhere.'

'Has she? – Then it is certain she is the one, the witch, the wife! It is her son who was cured a few months ago by Hogarth's magic. It must be the same young man!'

'Awfully far-fetched,' Caroline said. 'And, Willi, all this bores me.' In fact it agitated her, as he could see. 'That Hogarth crest,' she was thinking, 'on Eleanor's cigarette case. Laurence identified it, the same as Mrs Hogg's. ...' She decided to speak of this to Laurence later on.

Just then Helena shouted,

'Caroline, will you fetch my book – I threw it in at the back of the boot with my little head cushion. Will you fetch that too?'

'Hell!' Caroline breathed.

It meant unloading the entire contents of the boot. The

Baron helped Caroline to ease them out of the tiny space, while he talked as fast as he could, as if to get in as much as possible of his precious confidences in the next few moments.

'It is the same young man,' he said, 'and you will see that I am right.'

'You must be wrong,' said Caroline, out of breath with the effort of shifting the boxes, old petrol cans, and other clutter. She was reminding herself that only the other day Helena had said, 'Fancy, I told Mrs Hogg about that wonderful miracle that happened to the Hogarth boy. I thought it might give her some hope for her own son who's a cripple. But do you know, she wouldn't believe it was a miracle – she said if it had been a real miracle the young man would have become a Catholic. Unfortunately this Hogarth boy has gone off with some woman – a rich Theosophist, I understand. Perhaps I shouldn't have told Georgina that bit.'

'You must be wrong,' Caroline told the Baron. 'Helena knows Georgina Hogg's affairs. Ask Helena, she'll confirm that Mrs Hogg has nothing to do with Hogarth.' Again, she wondered about that crest.

'Helena does *not* know,' said the Baron. 'And another thing, Caroline. So exciting, Caroline. I am going to see Mervyn Hogarth this afternoon. I have been informed that he is staying at an Abbey a few miles from this spot. Now why should he be staying at a religious house? He must be posing as a Catholic retreatant. I daresay that these are the means he uses for stealing the consecrated elements for use in the Black Mass. After all, he must get them from somewhere –'

Caroline caught his sleeve and nodded towards the hedgerow a few yards from where the car was parked. He looked in that direction. The black hat had just bobbed out of sight.

'Mrs Hogg has been listening,' Caroline said in a loud voice.

'Did you call me, Miss Rose?'

Mrs Hogg came out of hiding as if she had never been in it.

'Lovely round here,' she said with her smile. 'Did you call? I thought you called "Mrs Hogg".'

Caroline walked away quickly, followed by the Baron, while Mrs Hogg made off along the towpath.

Caroline handed Helena the book. 'It had slipped down at the very back,' she said, 'I had to move everything. I feel as exhausted as if I'd done a hard day's work.'

'Oh, you shouldn't have – I thought Willi was doing all the heaving. Willi, why didn't you do all the heaving?'

'I did so, my Helena,' said the Baron.

'Mrs Hogg was bent behind the hedge listening to our conversation,' Caroline said.

'I take an oriental view of manual labour myself,' said Laurence. He was stretched in the dappling shade of a tree.

'She has nothing in her life,' Helena said, 'that's her trouble. She always has been a nosey type. Simply because she hasn't any life of her own. I'm sorry I brought her. I dread taking her back.'

Laurence gurgled. 'I think that's sweet.' Helena had not told him of their creepy experience with Georgina that morning.

'I've sent her off for a walk,' said Helena, looking round. 'I wonder if she'll be all right.' Georgina was nowhere in sight.

'Georgina is nowhere in sight,' she said anxiously.

'You've sent her off; well, she's gone off,' Laurence said. 'Stop jittering. Relax. Read your book. There's too much talking.'

'Which way did she go?' Helena said.

'Downstream, by the towpath,' said Caroline.

'Silence,' said Laurence. 'Let nothing disturb thee,' he chanted, 'nothing affright thee, all things are passing. . . .'

'God never changeth,' Helena continued, surprised that he had remembered the words.

The Baron was examining a map. 'I should be back just after four,' he said. 'Will that do?'

'Perfectly,' said Laurence. 'Kindly depart.'

'The Abbey is on the other side of the river,' said the Baron, 'but there's a bridge two miles down. I shall be back just after four.'

He set off with his jacket trailing over his arm. Lazily, they watched him until he was out of sight round a bend.

'I wonder why he wants to see the Abbey,' said Helena, 'it isn't an exceptional place, nothing architecturally speaking.'

'He's looking for a man he believes is staying at the Abbey. A man called Mervyn Hogarth,' Caroline said deliberately.

Helena looked startled. 'Mervyn Hogarth! Does Willi know him then?'

'By hearsay,' Caroline said.

'That's the father of the young man who was cured,' Helena said. 'Has Mr Hogarth become a Catholic, I wonder?'

'The Baron thinks,' Caroline said, 'that he is a magician. The Baron believes that Mervyn Hogarth is the leader of a Black Mass circle and that he's staying at the Abbey under the guise of a retreatant, but really on purpose to steal the consecrated Host.'

'Oh how frightful, oh how frightful!'

'The Baron has a kink,' Laurence put in.

'Exactly,' said Caroline.

'It does sound a far-fetched story,' Helena said. 'There's nothing in it, you think?'

'Nothing at all,' Caroline said. 'I should be surprised if he found Mervyn Hogarth at the Abbey. And more surprised if his suspicions were true.'

'It would be dreadful if they were true,' Helena said. 'But why should Willi Stock be troubled if they were; does he intend to expose the man?'

'No, he intends to write a monograph.'

Caroline put the palms of her hands out to the sun to get them browned.

'He thinks he is aloof from the subject of black magic, merely inter-ested. Whereas he is passionately attracted to it. "My nature,"' she quoted, ' "is subdued to what it works in, like the dyer's hand. Pity me then. . . ."'

'Willi always has been eccentric,' Helena remarked.

'Part of his cultivated Englishness,' said Laurence.

'It will be interesting,' Helena said, 'to hear what he says when he comes back.'

'Don't mention what I've told you,' Caroline said, 'he's touchy, poor Willi.'

She felt a sweet pleasure in her words, 'Poor Willi!' They soothed her resentment of the Baron's 'Poor Caroline!' with which he must have ended many an afternoon's session at Charing Cross Road. Especially with Helena was she pleased to discredit the Baron. Sometimes Helena would inquire gently of Caroline if she was quite happy – nothing worrying her? From which Caroline was sensitive to assume that the Baron had been talking. In fact, Helena had discouraged the Baron's gossip. One day in the early spring he had asked her plainly,

'Is it all off between Laurence and Caroline?'

'No, I don't think so. They are waiting.'

'For what? My dear, they are not chicks,' said the Baron.

'I suppose Caroline wants to get her book off her hands. But I don't know their business at all really. I wish they would do something definite, but there it is.'

'Caroline's "book",' he said; 'do you mean the book she is writing or the one in which she lives?'

'Now, Willi! Caroline is not a silly girl. She did have a little upset and imagined things, I know. And then there was the accident. But since that time she's recovered wonderfully.'

'*My* dear Helena, I do assure you that Caroline has been receiving communications from her Typing Spooks continuously since that time.'

'Nonsense. Caroline is perfectly sane. What's going to win the Lincoln, do you think, Willi?'

And so, occasionally, when Helena asked Caroline, 'Quite happy now, dear?' or 'Nothing worrying you?' Caroline would be unhappy and worrying about these inquiries.

So, on the day of the picnic she was especially happy to discuss the Baron's latest fantasy with Helena.

'He must have built up a theory,' said Helena, 'on rumours and suspicions. I hate,' she said with unusual force, 'doubt and suspicion.'

Caroline thought, 'She is worried about Mrs Hogg. The affair in the car is pressing on her mind. Poor Helena! Perhaps she would not at all like to know things clearly.'

Laurence lay listening to their voices, contentedly oblivious of what they said. He was too somnolent in the warmth of the sun to take part in the conversation and too enchanted by his sense of the summer day to waste it in sleep. He watched the movements of a young fat woman on a houseboat moored nearby. Every now and then she would disappear into the cabin to fetch something. First a bright scarf to protect her head from the sun. Then a cushion. Next she went below for so long a time, as it seemed to Laurence, that he thought she was never coming back. But she did emerge again, with a cup of tea. She drank it propped tubbily on the tiny bridge of the boat. Laurence spent his pleasurable idleness of long meaningless moments in following every sip. He wished the houseboat were his. He wondered where the man of the house could be, for he was sure there must be a man, referred to by Tubby as 'my friend'. Laurence wished it were possible for him to go on lying drowsily by the river and at the same time to poke about in the cabin of the boat, to pry into the cooking arrangements, the bunks, the engine. A little rowing boat which lay alongside caught Laurence's fancy.

It came home to him that Caroline was saying, 'I'll start the kettle for tea.'

She had lit the spirit stove when Helena said, 'Thunder.'

'No,' said Laurence. 'Couldn't be. I was just thinking,' he said, 'we might be able to borrow that little boat and row over to the other side.'

'*I* thought I heard a rumble,' Caroline said.

'No.'

'It's quarter past four,' Helena said. 'I wonder where Georgina has got to?'

'Spirited away,' said Laurence remarkably.

Helena roused him to scout round for Georgina.

'I'm sure it's going to rain,' she said.

The sky had clouded, and in spite of Laurence's protests the barking of distant thunder was undeniable.

'The thunder's miles away over the downs,' Laurence said, 'it will miss the valley.' Nevertheless, he went off in search of Mrs Hogg, pausing on the way to look more closely at the houseboat. The plump girl had gone inside.

Caroline and Helena started to move their rugs and tea-cups into the cars.

'Even if we miss the storm,' Helena said, 'it will certainly set in to rain within the next ten minutes.'

Suddenly they caught sight of the Baron on the opposite bank. He shouted something, but he was too far from them to be heard. With his hands describing a circuit he conveyed that he was coming back by the bridge.

'He'll get soaked,' Caroline said. 'Poor Willi!' But before he set off again she waved him to stop.

'I'll ask for the boat,' she said, 'and row him over.'

'That *would* be nice,' Helena said. 'Sure you can manage it?'

But Caroline, with Laurence's raincoat over her shoulders, was away to the houseboat. The Baron stood perplexed for a moment. He saw Caroline bend down and knock at the little window. He understood the plan, then, and waited. In a few minutes Caroline signed to him that she had the owner's permission to use the boat.

The rain had started, but it was light and the river calm. Caroline reached him within a few moments. He climbed into the boat and took the oars from her.

'I got a sight of Hogarth,' he said immediately, 'alias Hogg, but he was in disguise. Quite a different appearance from the man I saw conducting the Black Mass. In the circumstances I did not address him, it was too frightening.'

'How did you know it was Mervyn Hogarth, then?'

'I asked one of the lay-brothers. He confirmed that Mervyn Hogarth was staying there, and pointed him out. *They* believe he is come to the Abbey for the fishing.'

'What fishing?'

'Apparently the Abbey rents out a strip of fishing ground. They put up the anglers in the Abbey,' said the Baron. 'Little do they know whom they are harbouring. Hogarth alias Hogg,' he said.

'I think you are mixed up, Willi.' Caroline pulled the raincoat over her head and patted her hair beneath it. 'The man at the Black Mass must have been a different Hogarth.'

'Oh no, *he* was named Hogg. Hogarth is the daytime name. I know for a fact that Mervyn Hogarth was born Mervyn Hogg.'

'The man at the Black Mass must have been a different Hogg.'

'I have the whole picture, which you have not,' the Baron said. 'This afternoon, as I was leaving the Abbey grounds I saw the witch, Mrs Hogg, entering them. I turned back and followed her. I *saw* – actually saw, Caroline – Mrs Hogg approaching Hogarth. He was doing something to a fishing rod at the time. He recognized her of course. He looked very miserable. They exchanged a few words. Soon, he walked away and left her. The couple are clearly known to each other.'

They had landed. Caroline thanked the woman while the Baron tied up the boat.

'There's no sign of Georgina,' Helena said as they reached her car. 'Laurence has been back and he's gone off again to search for her. What a nuisance.'

'She was over at the Abbey,' said the Baron. 'I left her there half an hour ago.'

'How vexing. Well, we shall have to wait. Let's try and continue some tea in the back of the car.'

The thunder was still distant. The storm that was raging some miles away seemed unlikely to reach them, but now the rain was heavy.

'Which way did Laurence go?' the Baron said.

'Towards the bridge.'

'I'll take his car and meet him. I daresay I shall pick up Mrs Hogg on her way back. She must be at the bridge by now.'

He drove off. Every few minutes Helena poked her head out of the back window of her car. 'I hope they don't miss each other,' she said, 'Laurence only has his jacket. Oh, there's Georgina!'

Mrs Hogg was coming down to the riverside by a track through the trees on the opposite bank. She saw Helena and raised her hand in recognition.

Helena made a frantic dumb-show at her. Mrs Hogg stood waiting and stupid-looking.

'Caroline,' said Helena, 'be an angel.'

'You want me to fetch her in the boat,' Caroline stated.

'Put the mac over your head, do.' Helena was nervy. 'We shall be kept waiting here for ages if she has to plod round by the bridge. It's two miles each way. I'm dying to get home.'

When Caroline did not reply, Helena seemed aware of having asked more than an ordinary favour.

'I'll go, dear,' said Helena at once. 'Give me the mac. I'm sure I can manage the boat.'

Caroline was sure she couldn't. She jumped out of the car and was off like someone taking a plunge against nature.

In spite of the rain, with only a cardigan over her summer dress, Helena followed. She caught up Caroline at the houseboat, and added her gracious thanks to the owner. As Caroline unmoored she said,

'This really is charitable, Caroline. Poor Georgina would be drenched if she had to walk round to cross the bridge.'

Caroline gave her an amiable smile, for she was too proud to reveal her neurotic dread. Her dread was on account of a very small thing. She knew she would have to give Mrs Hogg a hand into the boat. The anticipation of this physical contact, her hand in Mrs Hogg's only for a moment, horrified Caroline. It was a very small thing, but it was what she constitutionally dreaded.

'Step down here, Mrs Hogg. On to that stone. Give me your hand. Take care, the river's deep here.'

The bank had grown muddy but there were several firm footholds. Caroline, standing astride in the boat, reached out and grasped Mrs Hogg's hand firmly. Step there, now there. 'I'm doing fine,' Caroline thought, gripping the woman's hand tightly in her own. She was filled with the consciousness of hand.

Mrs Hogg had rubber-soled shoes which had picked up a good deal of mud. In spite of all her care she slipped on her heels, she tottered backwards with her hand still gripped in Caroline's so that the boat rocked wildly. In an instant she was loudly in the water and Caroline, still grasping the hand by the first compulsive need to over-come her horror of it, went with her. Mrs Hogg lashed about her in a screaming panic. Caroline freed herself and gripped the side of the boat. But she was wrenched away, the woman's hands were on her neck – 'I can't swim!'

Caroline struck her in the face. 'Hold on to my shoulders,' she shouted. 'I can swim.' But the woman in her extremity was intent on Caroline's throat. Caroline saw the little boat bobbing away downstream. Then her sight became blocked by one of Mrs Hogg's great hands clawing across her eyes, the other hand tightening on her throat. Mrs Hogg's body, and even legs, encompassed Caroline so that her arms were restricted. She knew then that if she could not free herself from Mrs Hogg they would both go under.

They were under water and out of sight for a while. Helena said later that it was only a matter of seconds before Caroline's head emerged. But in that space of time it was a long breath-holding contest between them. Caroline had practised underwater swimming. Not so, Mrs Hogg. The woman clung to Caroline's throat until the last. It was not until Mrs Hogg opened her mouth finally to the inrush of water that her grip slackened and Caroline was free, her lungs aching for the breath of life. Mrs Hogg subsided away from her. God knows where she went.

Caroline had the sense of being hauled along a bumpy surface, of being landed with a thud like a gasping fish, before she passed out.

'Jolly good luck I had my friend here. I can't swim myself.'

Caroline lay in the bunk of the houseboat, without a sense or even a care of where she was. She recognized Helena, then the plump woman of the houseboat and a strange man who was taking off all his dripping wet clothes. Caroline had a sense of childhood, and she closed her eyes.

'There was no sign of the other,' the man was saying. 'She's had it. Any relation?'

'No,' said Helena's voice.

'She gave this one a rough time,' said the man. 'Just look at her face. I'll bet she's been trained to hold her breath under water. If she hadn't, she'd have had it too, this one.'

The woman of the houseboat helped Caroline to sip from a warm beaker.

'Have you anything to put on the scratches?' That was Helena.

Presently Caroline felt something soft being smoothed

over her face and throat. Her neck was hurting. And again she was sipping something warm and sweet, her shoulders supported by Helena.

The man said, 'I had a look for the other, best I could. It's deep in that spot. I daresay we'll get the body. There was a tragedy five summers back and we got the body two days after.'

Helena murmured, 'You've been marvellous.'

Before she went off to sleep, Caroline heard Laurence's voice from somewhere outside, then the Baron's, then Helena again,

'Here they are with the doctor.'

Sir Edwin Manders was making his autumn retreat. October 24th, the Feast of St Raphael the Archangel; he had arrived at the monastery during the afternoon in time for Benediction.

The window of his room looked down on a green courtyard over which the leaves were scattering. Fixing his eye on this sunlit square of leaves and grass, he gave himself to think about his surprising family affairs.

Usually when he was in retreat this man would give his time, under a spiritual director, to regarding the state of his soul. In the past few months he had been given cause to wonder if he did not make his retreats too frequently. Amazing things occurred at home; extraordinary events which he never heard of till later.

'Why didn't you inform me at the time, Helena?'

'You were in retreat, Edwin.'

He had misgivings then, about his retreats. He told his spiritual director. 'I might have done better to spend the time at home. My family have had to cope with difficulties ... my son ... my brother ... my mother-in-law ... one of our old servants ... I might have done better had I not made so many retreats.'

'You might have done worse,' said the shrewd old priest, and sounded as if he meant it. It was a humiliating thought, which in turn was good for the soul.

'They manage admirably without me,' Edwin Manders admitted.

And so he was in retreat again. Really on this occasion he had not wanted to come. But Helena insisted. Ernest even, in his shy way, had said, 'Someone has got to pray for us, Edwin.' Laurence had said, 'Cancel your autumn retreat? Oh you can't do that,' without giving any reasons. Caroline Rose had driven him to the station.

For years he had felt drawn to the contemplative life. To partake more fully of it he had retired, all but nominally, from Manders' Figs. Helena took pride in his frequent recourse to monasteries. In fact he was embarrassed at this moment to realize how effectively she had fostered the legend of his 'certain sanctity'. More and more he had felt attracted by the ascetic formalities. Only this autumn, in his hesitation before leaving home, did he feel he was being pushed into it.

He had no more qualms after his arrival at the monastery. The charm began to work on him. His austere cell was like a drug. The rise and fall of plain-song from the Chapel invited him into its abiding pure world. The noiseless, timeless lay-brothers moved amenably about their business, causing Edwin Manders to feel pleasurably humble in the presence of this profound elect. The fact that there was a big upset going on in the monastic quarters of the buildings due to half the bedrooms being flooded by a burst pipe, that one of the lay-brothers was sick to death of his life, that the Abbot was worried about an overdraft, was mercifully concealed from Edwin at that moment. And so he was sufficiently unhampered by material distractions to see his spiritual temptation plain, which being so, he found it after all resistable, that luxurious nostalgia, that opium daze of devotion, for he knew, more or less, that he never would have made a religious. He gave his mind to reviewing his family affairs.

There were two items in the embarrassing category, for both had reached the newspapers. He was in doubt which was the more distressing, Louisa Jepp's case or Georgina Hogg's. He decided, on the whole, Georgina's. And for a good half-hour he concentrated on Georgina, now lodged, it was believed, in the mud of the Medway, for her body was never recovered. There was a piece in the London evening papers, mentioning by name Helena, Laurence, Caroline, Baron Stock, and the couple on the houseboat. There was an inquest. Poor Helena. In former days, he recalled, their name for Georgina in the household was Manders' Mortification.

As he heard afterwards, for he was in retreat at the time, Helena got Laurence to make inquiries for poor Mrs Hogg's son. He turned out to be an unfortunate person. The father a bigamist. Helena dropped her inquiries as soon as she learned that Eleanor Hogarth was involved in the bigamy; innocently no doubt, but she was in partnership with his brother Ernest, another embarrassment ... Helena hushed it up. Helena was marvellous.

'We had a sort of forewarning of Mrs Hogg's death. Willi Stock and I were on our way to the picnic, with Georgina at the back. . . .'

Women were rather fanciful, of course. Edwin often wondered if there was any truth in the story that Mrs Hogg's son was miraculously cured. Helena was convinced of it. There had been nothing official on the subject. The man in question had been taken under the wing of a wealthy woman, a Theist or Theosophist, something like that. Anyway, the later news was that he had left that woman's house and departed for Canada to lecture there about his cure.

'In spite of which,' Edwin thought, 'young Hogarth may be a worthier man than me.'

Likewise, when he turned to Baron Stock, he murmured, '*Miserere mei, Deus.*' The Baron, probably a better man than himself, was having treatment in a private mental home and, according to accounts, loving it. He thought of his brother Ernest, so worldly and yet so short of money and not perhaps really keen on that dancing girl. He forced himself to consider Eleanor.... 'All these people have suffered while I have fattened on fasting.' He meant what he said, and so truly he was not as limited as he seemed.

And to think of his mother-in-law! He reflected, now, unflinchingly on the question of Louisa Jepp. There again he could not quite grasp ... smuggling diamonds, a gang, it sounded like an adventure story. Then there was Louisa's real folly and it was quite embarrassing. Heroically he forced his mind to that moment in September when, at breakfast, Helena limply passed him a letter. The letter was from Louisa. With it was a press cutting from a local paper. The press cutting was headed 'Sunset Wedding'. It was a long piece. It began 'In the sunset of their lives two of the old folks of Ladylees have come together in Holy Matrimony. At all Saints' on Saturday last, Mrs Louisa Jepp, 78, of Smugglers' Retreat, Ladylees, gave her hand in marriage to Mr J. G. L. Webster, 77, of the Old Mill, Ladylees. ... The bride promised to "obey". ...' This was followed by a substantial account of Webster and his career in the Merchant Navy, and the column ended, 'Mrs Jepp (now Webster) has one daughter, Lady Manders, wife of Sir Edwin Manders, head of the famous firm Manders' Figs in Syrup. The Rev. R. Socket who conducted the ceremony stated, "This is a very happy and unique occasion. Though not a regular churchgoer, Mrs Jepp is a figure much loved and respected in the district." '

The accompanying letter was brief. In it Louisa remarked, 'It is not strictly accurate to say that I am not a regular churchgoer as I go to church regularly on Remembrance Day.'

'It isn't for us to judge her wisdom,' Helena said glumly.

Edwin stared out at the green quadrangle, the blown leaves. *Miserere nobis.* . . . Have mercy.

Laurence and Caroline had been high-spirited about Louisa's marriage. That was to be expected of Laurence.

201

He had always adored his grandmother; and indeed she was charming, indeed.

Edwin wondered if Caroline herself was really interested in marriage.

'She's waiting for Laurence to return to the Church,' Helena said.

He wondered. Caroline was an odd sort of Catholic, very little heart for it, all mind.

'That dreadful experience with poor Georgina in the river hasn't had any harmful effects on Caroline,' Helena said. 'She must have a strong constitution. In fact, since then she's been much more lighthearted. She seems to be amused by something, I don't know what.'

Caroline had finished her book about novels. Now she announced she was going away on a long holiday. She was going to write a novel.

'I don't call that a holiday,' said Helena, 'not if you mean to spend it writing a novel.'

'This is a holiday of obligation,' Caroline replied.

'What is the novel to be about?'

Caroline answered, 'Characters in a novel.'

Edwin himself had said, 'Make it a straight old-fashioned story, no modern mystifications. End with the death of the villain and the marriage of the heroine.'

Caroline laughed and said, 'Yes, it would end that way.'

A few weeks later the character called Laurence Manders was snooping around in Caroline Rose's flat. She was away in Worcestershire writing her novel, and he had gone to the flat to collect some books which she had asked to be sent to her.

He took his time. In fact, the books were the last things he looked for.

He thought, 'What am I looking for?' and flicked the dresses in her wardrobe.

He found the books that Caroline wanted, but before he left he sat down at Caroline's desk and wrote her a letter.

I have spent 2 hours 28 mins. in your flat [he wrote]. I have found those books for you, and had a look round. Why did you lock the right-hand drawer in the wall cupboard? I had difficulty in getting it open, and then the hair curlers in one box and the scarves in another, and the white gloves were all I found. I can't lock it again. I have just found myself wondering what I was looking for.

I found an enormous sheaf of your notes for your novel in the cupboard in that carton marked Keep in a Cool Place. Why did you leave them behind? What's the point of making notes if you don't use them while you are writing the book?

Do you want me to send the notes to you?

I wonder if you left them on purpose, so that I should read them?

But I remember your once saying you always made a lot of notes for a book, then never referred to them. I feel very niggled.

I will tell you what I think of your notes:

(1) You misrepresent all of us.
(2) Obviously you are the martyr-figure. 'Martyrdom by misunderstanding.' But actually you yourself understand nobody, for instance the Baron, my father, myself, we are martyred by your misunderstanding.
(3) I love you. I think you are hopelessly selfish.
(4) I dislike being a character in your novel. How is it all going to end?

Laurence wrote a long letter, re-read it, then folded and sealed it. He put it in his pocket, stacked away Caroline's notes in their place in the carton in the cupboard.

The autumn afternoon was darkening as he turned into Hampstead Heath. Religion had so changed Caroline. At one time he had thought it would make life easier for her, and indirectly for himself. 'You have to be involved personally,' Caroline had said on one occasion, infuriating him by the know-all assumption of the words. At least, he thought, I am honest; I misunderstand Caroline. His letter had failed to express his objections. He took it out of his pocket and tore it up into small pieces, scattering them over the Heath where the wind bore them away.

He saw the bits of paper come to rest, some on the scrubby ground, some among the deep marsh weeds, and one piece on a thorn-bush; and he did not then foresee his later wonder, with a curious rejoicing, how the letter had got into the book.

THE REVIVED MODERN CLASSICS

Sherwood Anderson, *Poor White* • **H.E. Bates,** *A Month by the Lake & Other Stories. A Party for the Girls. Elephant's Nest in a Rhubarb Tree* • **Kay Boyle,** *Death of a Man. Fifty Stories. Life Being the Best & Other Stories. Three Short Novels* • **Mikhail Bulgakov,** *The Life of Monsieur de Molière* • **Joyce Cary,** The Second Trilogy: *Prisoner of Grace, Except the Lord, Not Honour More. A House of Children. Mister Johnson* • **Maurice Collis,** *The Land of the Great Image. She Was a Queen* • **Shusaku Endo,** *The Sea & Poison. Stained Glass Elegies* • **Ronald Firbank,** *Three More Novels* • **Romain Gary,** *The Life Before Us. Promise at Dawn* • **William Gerhardie,** *Futility* • **Dezsö Kosztolányi,** *Anna Édes* • **Madame de Lafayette,** *The Princess of Cleves* • **Siegfried Lenz,** *The German Lesson* • **Henri Michaux,** *A Barbarian in Asia* • **Henry Miller,** *Aller Retour New York* • **Vladimir Nabokov,** *Laughter in the Dark* • **Eça de Queirós,** *The Illustrious House of Ramires* • **Raymond Queneau,** *The Blue Flowers* • **Kenneth Rexroth,** *An Autobiographical Novel. Classics Revisited. More Classics Revisited* • **William Saroyan,** *The Man with the Heart in the Highlands & Other Early Stories* • **Muriel Spark,** *The Public Image. The Comforters* • **Stevie Smith,** *Novel on Yellow Paper* • **Stendhal,** *Three Italian Chronicles* • **Niccolò Tucci,** *The Rain Came Last & Other Stories* • **Robert Penn Warren,** *At Heaven's Gate.*